THE VIGILANTE'S LOVER

VOL. 3

Annie Winters
Tony West

www.anniewinters.com
www.tonywestwrites.com

casey shay press

Casey Shay Press
PO Box 160116
Austin, TX 78716
www.caseyshaypress.com

ISBN: 9781938150456

Also available in digital format.
eISBN: 9781938150401

Library of Congress Control Number: 2015932791

FIRST EDITION

Also by Annie Winters

Writing as JJ Knight
The UNCAGED LOVE Series
The FIGHT FOR HER Series

Writing as Deanna Roy
Forever Innocent
Forever Loved
Forever Sheltered

Learn about appearances and events at
www.deannaroy.com

For our TEAM who makes everything come together:

Dana, we could not go a day without you
Marianne, you never laugh at our typos
Aubrey, those amazing covers, WOW
Carina, behind the scenes CreateSpace MAGIC

1

JAX

The explosion rocks the house and my first thought — and hopefully not my last — is Mia. She's going to panic.

The reverberations continue as the house shudders, wood splintering, chaos raining down.

But I'm glad I caught my mistake in time to get behind a steel door. This building is full of them, being a safe house.

But I'm still seething at Klaus and Jovana.

The knot was a trick.

It wasn't a blood knot. The trigger was made of

completely different ropes. It took my adjusting the tension to notice the trick, and by then the coils had already released.

Very clever, Klaus.

I clutch the handle on the reinforced door, glad I was familiar with the safe house and its protected spaces. I go over the bomb's working again in my mind. What had they wanted to happen? Mia to die? Me? Both? Then why the smaller bombs on the way in?

They hadn't wanted me to escape. Maybe they thought Mia and I would work on this one together, and they would get us both. Mia *had* tied Klaus up. They knew she was well versed in knots.

To do it alone, I had to clutch the two ends of rope together, my hand serving the role of the fake coils. The barest perceptible click from the other side of the door told me the bomb had been tripped. I knew that if I let go, the sudden loss of tension would set it off immediately. Pulling the ropes too far from the door would do the same.

Still, I couldn't just tie the two ropes back together. There was no telling what was attached to the lower line, and I dared not test the amount of free slack I had left in the top line. I also couldn't stay by the bedroom door forever.

What saved me was realizing that I needed something to replace my hand. To hold the tension long enough for me to get away.

I looked around at the hall. Nothing was within reach, except what I had on me. But that included a shoe.

Carefully I shucked one of them off and weighed it in my free hand. On its own I feared it was too light, but with its mate I knew it just might be enough. I lifted my leg, removed the other shoe, then tied them together. It would have to do.

My question was, as I held that weighted string in my hand, waiting for the bomb — was the reinforced room at the end of the hall strong enough to survive the force of the explosion?

I'm still waiting on that. More debris rains down. I push on the side of the closet and feel it give. The connecting wall has probably collapsed. I'm safe here for the moment, so I wait a little longer for the house to settle. It won't help to survive the blast just to have the roof collapse on top of me when I try to leave.

It was a good bomb, probably the best I've seen Klaus do, since he's not an ammunitions man. If I'd misjudged Klaus's handiwork, it would have gone off almost immediately. But I was right, and I bought myself a few precious seconds as the weight of the shoes kept the line taut.

When I let go of the line, I didn't wait to see the results and instead raced down the hall to the linen closet. I yanked the door open just as Mia's voice started bellowing from the camera in my pocket. I had no time to answer. I shoved myself inside.

I almost didn't get the door closed in time.

I felt the explosion through the floor a fraction of a second before I heard it. A blast of heat and force pushed its way through the gap in the door as I slammed it closed. Even inside the reinforced walls the sound was deafening. The walls shuddered and vibrated with the impact and I was flung back. I felt the crack of my video cam as I hit the wall, and Mia's voice ceased.

Now that the worst of the crisis is over, I pull the video chat device out to examine the damage. The little screen is cracked and black. I push the buttons but get nothing. It's completely inoperable. Mia will panic and run toward me. I know it.

And there are five working land mines still out in the field. I only disarmed one on the way in.

The urgency to get out obliterates everything else.

Don't come toward me, Mia, I silently insist.

Wait by the car. Wait by the car.

I press my hands to the door. The metal panel is slightly bowed but otherwise intact. I wrench it open and peer out. Where Mia's room had been is nothing but a gaping hole looking out into the front yard. The hallway is scorched and filled with debris. Parts of the walls are missing. Bits of roofing and insulation hang down like old party decorations. The windows have been blown out.

I can't see out the back. Enough of the walls are standing that the fields and the car where Mia waits aren't visible from my viewpoint.

Surely she'll wait by the car. Surely.

I take a tentative step out, making sure the floor is sound, then push through the mess to find a way out.

Then I hear it.

An explosion outside.

The land mines.

"Mia!" I shout, and crash through the debris.

2

MIA

Oh God, oh God, oh God.

I have to get to the house. Jax is hurt. Maybe dead.

Oh God.

The round hay bale that hit the land mine is still partially intact. I think I can make it roll again. If I keep pushing it ahead of me and letting it set off the bombs, maybe I can get to the house. And Jax.

He could be dying in there. I picture his body on the floor. His face contorted in pain.

I have to get inside.

I push the tattered remains of the hay bale ahead of me. Now that I've seen how much explosive power the land mine has, I'm less afraid. If I can just get this bundle close to the next bale, I'll be halfway to the house.

The hay is a lot harder to roll now that it's less round, but it's also half the weight. I shove it hard, keeping it a little ahead of me. I reach a small dip in the field, and another big push sends it straight for the next one.

Then it blows again.

Damn it. There's too much distance between where it went off and the next hay bale. I can't go any farther. The next land mine could be in my path.

I stare at the house, so afraid for Jax that I want to collapse to the ground. The side wall has caved in, and part of the roof has blown on top of the rest. I know the front must have fared even worse than the back, since he was outside my bedroom and it looked out on the road.

The temptation to run is so bad, so bad. I snatch the video cam from my pajama-top pocket. I push the button again and again to call him.

Still nothing but static.

If it was destroyed, how could Jax have possibly survived? He was holding it.

I'm so stuck. I can't walk any closer to the house.

I can go back to the car, but then what? Roll Jax's Aston Martin ahead of me to let it take the bombs?

Maybe.

I try to picture Jax walking to the house. What spots did he avoid? Did he zigzag as he avoided the mines? He bent down at one point, probably looking at one. If only he had two of whatever gadget told him where they were. I could use it now.

Maybe I should just go back to the car. Call for help. The fire department. He'll need medical attention anyway. Maybe we can lie about who he is, and the Vigilantes won't catch him.

I've never been in any situation like this.

Think, Mia. Don't panic.

Then I see it.

The back door. It moves.

At first it just shifts a little. Then it falls flat onto the back porch.

And I see him.

Jax.

He's not dead!

I almost run forward, then halt. The mines.

"Jax!" I cry out. "You made it!"

He holds out his arms as if to say, "Of course I did."

Jax walks with certainty toward me. He's not scanning anything. Has he forgotten?

"Jax! The land mines!"

"I remember!" he calls out. He steps to the left, and I realize he has their position in his head. He somehow knows exactly where they are from when he scanned them before.

I am in awe of him. I don't know if I can ever be that good. It's my own field, and still, I couldn't remember the direction that he walked or what part he avoided on the way in.

But he does.

He pauses by the wreckage of the hay bale. "That was incredibly clever," he says.

"What, destroying the hay?"

"Yes. Brilliant idea."

"It didn't get me to the house."

He looks back at it. "Your home is destroyed."

"Won't the fire department be here soon? We should go."

His eyes search mine. "It's your home."

I look across the field. "Not anymore."

"There isn't anything you want from it?"

I think of the photos of my parents. My aunt's silver bells. Where would I put them if I took them?

"You have your phone?" I ask him. "Does it work? The video stopped."

He pulls the video cam from his pocket. "This is broken, but I have other things in the car."

I turn away from the smoking remains of my aunt's house. "I'm going to call my neighbor and tell her I'm all right. She'll pick up the few mementos that matter to me."

Jax nods. His face is streaked with ash and his impeccable suit shirt and gray pants are frayed and covered in soot. His shoes are missing. But he looks amazing.

"Let's get out of here before law enforcement shows," he says. "No doubt they've been called by now." He passes me his bag, which has seen better days, dirty and torn. "We'll have our land mine lesson later. Right now I'm going to disarm the last ones so no firefighters come across them."

"Klaus would have let innocent people get hurt by them?"

A dark expression crosses his face. "Not the Klaus I knew. But now?" His voice trails off.

He strides back into the field. I hug his bag to my chest, smelling smoke and charred wood coming from it. I know Jax is upset about his friend. Someone he once trusted is now his absolute worst enemy.

3

JAX

Mia looks exhausted as we drive toward Nashville. She called her neighbor, who tried to insist Mia come over and stay with her. Mia managed to convince her she was already gone but would come back someday.

She's mine now. I feel responsible for what happened. I wrote the letters to the safe house and didn't recognize what was really going on with the garbled replies.

I came, and I brought the danger to her.

Twice the Vigilantes have almost killed her.

I can't let that happen.

She watches the trees pass by outside the window, lost in thought. I wonder what is going on inside her head. Regrets over what she's been through since she met me?

Her chin is high, strong even with all this terror. Something in my chest turns a little. She's brave. Tougher than I gave her credit for that first night.

I'm disgusted by my own network. I don't know what is going on for them to decide to destroy her house. Vigilantes are not heroes by any means, but we are law enforcers in our own right. We just no longer trust the civilian system of police, judges, and justice that goes to the highest bidder.

We use vastly advanced technology and financial resources to find the truth in ways that aren't practical or legal. And our retribution is swift and final.

But Mia is an innocent woman. And they are allowing her to get caught in the crossfire. My crossfire.

I send an encrypted message to Sam about the whereabouts of the Vigilante car I stole from the idiot who tried to take me down in Albuquerque.

Having a vehicle like that will be a bonus for Sam to play with. He can break it down and build it back up into an amazing machine.

I feel confident in my own Aston Martin. This car is completely off grid and always has been, one of the perks of being a director of a silo, like I once was.

Before I killed a Vigilante.

Before I believed that damn woman.

Jovana's going to have the surprise of her life when she sees me at her brother's fight in Nashville. Klaus too.

They aren't going to know what hit them.

But first, we have to get clothes, food, rest. We have two days to kill until then. We've been way beyond the basics for days, and Mia isn't used to this lifestyle. I kept her up half the night.

I glance at her again as I think about the motel. She has hay stuck to her pajamas from the explosions. I've put her through the wringer, that's for certain.

I don't know what she's feeling about what happened. She's bound to be sore in places she didn't know existed. Probably I should have stayed away from her.

But some things you just can't help.

She's barely keeping her eyes open as we glide along the highway. Once we get to Nashville, I'll bring this down a notch, give us some quiet time. Maybe I can learn more about her, figure out what in her history would bring out these opposites in the Vigilantes, both naming her a special and allowing Jovana to destroy her home.

We'll be flying blind. I have to stay off grid. And I can't check into any of my usual places due to the kill order. But there are plenty of fine hotels in Nashville. My funds are well hidden. The Vigilantes can only seize what they know about. We're expected to funnel money all over the world.

I punch the search function on the dash. I admire for a moment the elegant controls in polished steel with inlaid teak. My car. I can't believe I have it back.

"Five-star hotel in Nashville," I tell it.

A list pops up and I choose one I've never been to before. There won't be a back entrance or my usual amenities. But it's a definite improvement over a barn and a seedy motel.

I think of the leisurely evening I can spend with Mia and my groin tightens. I book a room and tap in a request for top floor only. I select every VIP option that exists and a time of arrival. To keep them guessing, I list an assumed name with the word Viscount in front.

Even though it is midafternoon, Mia falls asleep, her arms and head draped over the center console. Her golden brown hair falls across her face. I catch myself about to move it, and pull back. It's one thing to keep her now, but I'm not going to be so foolish as to get emotional about it.

Emotion is what got me here.

Besides, eventually I will have to turn her over to the Vigilantes, so they will stop putting her in danger trying to get to me. I'll tell them I kidnapped her again. Whatever I have to say.

Maybe if I can clear my name, get to the endgame of whatever plot is unfolding, I can find my way back to her. But once I get to Jovana and Klaus again, I have to let her go. Get her out of harm's way.

But not tonight.

Screw it. I finger the loose bit of hair and slip it behind her ear. Her cheek is soft, her expression relaxed. I'll set up some spa treatment for her to get past the shock of these days. I'll watch each delicious moment as she gets a full body massage.

I tap the dash screen again and bring up Armond. It takes a few moments for the circuitous encryption to make its way to him. His bald head and bushy brows are a welcoming sight.

"You're still with us," he says. "I hear there's trouble afoot. Did you find your lady?"

I lay a hand on Mia's head. He looks down and sees her.

"Wearing them out as usual," he says, then nods knowingly when I glare at him. "Ah, you care what this little dove thinks of you."

"They blew up her house. She's got nothing to wear. Not even a hairbrush. What can you do for her?"

Armond's hands come up, his fingertips to his chin. "Now that is a tragedy. But we shall rebuild her from scratch. How much time?"

"We can rendezvous somewhere mid-Tennessee."

"There's a small college in Jackson," Armond says. "My very own nephew attends. There is a coffee shop in town with a name that will make your blood boil. Very defendable. When?"

I glance at the map. "Two hours normal speed.

Trying to stay under the radar."

"Plenty of time," he says. "Take care, my friend."

Mia pops her head up. She was listening. I figured as much.

"No stilettos!" she says.

Armond laughs. "No movie heroine here, I see, all high heels and dramatic hair amid the gunfire."

"I'll be the practical kind," Mia says. Her affection for Armond is obvious in her pleased expression. "Hair back. Body armor. And sensible shoes."

"I'll see what I can do. But perhaps one small addition, for the bedroom?"

Mia's face turns crimson.

"Ah, sorry, I should not be so coarse," he says. "My apologies."

"Good-bye, Armond," I say. "And thank you." I switch off the screen.

Mia sighs. "Do you sleep with EVERY woman you encounter?"

I exit the highway to take the back roads to Jackson. "I missed out on this eighty-year-old woman in Romania —"

"Jax! Don't be mean!"

I can barely contain my laugh. "I tried! She said I needed more potatoes first."

She punches my arm, and I trap her hand inside the crook of my elbow. I set the car to auto-navigate the narrow two-lane road and hold her fingers with mine.

Her eyes glow a little when I touch her. Just the way I like it. I wonder when I will move us to the next level, beyond the simple bedroom activities and on to those with a little more kick. Something tells me Mia is going to be very receptive.

Maybe tonight.

She drops her head back to the console, letting me stroke her fingers. I look forward to this night together, pushing her, seeing how far she bends.

Nothing's broken her so far.

4

MIA

Arriving at this fancy hotel will be nothing like the last.

For one, I'm not tied up in ropes. It's not the middle of the night. And there's no back entrance with people who know who Jax is. We're having to arrive under a false name.

Thankfully, I don't have to show up in my hay-covered pajamas. We met with Armond's nephew Brink at a coffee shop in some small town on the way. He was loaded down with two enormous suitcases of clothes and shoes and a dizzying array of shampoos, skin creams, and girly accessories.

Including a pair of over-the-knee black leather stiletto boots with peekaboo toes.

That Armond.

Jax hadn't been able to tell me the name of our stop until he suddenly jerked the car off the road and pulled into a place called "Carly's Joe." He scowled like the sign was a grave insult, but when I asked him about it, all he said was "I used to know a Carly in Vegas, and 'Ho' would be a better name." That's all I could get out of him.

I can't imagine any woman doing anything but swooning for Jax, but then there's this Jovana woman. She's trying to get him killed.

Although sometimes, I understand that impulse too.

I sort through my suitcase in the coffee shop bathroom and select a soft pair of jeans and a bright emerald sweater. A pair of navy ballerina flats make me feel normal again. I do sort of miss the Phase One trainee shoes that are now probably bits of leather and circuits in my blown-up bedroom.

My first act of Vigilantism and it's gone forever.

Jax seems relaxed as we navigate through Nashville and pull into the valet circle of a sprawling hotel. He's back in one of the fancy suits I'm used to seeing him in. Armond provided for him as well. This one is charcoal gray with the thinnest stripes.

As we drive, though, he sheds the suit jacket and tosses it in the back. With his shirt unbuttoned at the throat and his sleeves rolled up to his elbow, he looks almost casual.

He catches me watching and nods in acknowledgment of my attention. It isn't exactly a loving gesture, but I'll take it. Jax doesn't smile at much, and I'm just so glad I'm here that I won't ask for anything more.

Pulling up to a hotel makes my stomach flutter. I have a little better idea about what's going to happen now.

My pulse jumps as I think about the night before with Jax. The blood rushing down low brings out the mild ache. That soreness is nothing, though, compared to what I want to feel. Even the books I've read couldn't do justice to actually living it.

His attention is focused as he drops the car into park, scanning the doors, the doormen, no doubt watching for abnormalities and scanning for threats. Then his eyes rest on me and he calms.

This makes my stomach settle. I'm good for him. He doesn't know it yet, or won't admit it. But I can see it.

The valet opens his door, and a young man in a uniform starts pulling the suitcases from the trunk. We are barely through the hotel entrance when we're stopped by an older gentleman in a suit.

"Viscount Argetti," he says smoothly. "We've arranged for an early dinner in your room, plus the champagne you asked for. Here is your key and the elevator pass to the executive floor. Please let me know if I can be of any assistance." He bows like Jax is some sort of royalty.

"There is one small matter," Jax says.

"Anything, sir." The man seems eager to hear.

"I'd appreciate it if we were allowed to use an exit that is less," Jax glances at the glass entrance to the hotel, "public."

"Certainly, sir," the man says. "Just ring me and ask for an escort. I'll send our most discreet security to show you out."

"Thank you," Jax says. "It is a load off my mind, as my wife here is expecting and we would like to avoid any stress."

The man bows again. "Then congratulations, sir. We will do our utmost to prevent anyone from noticing your arrivals or departures."

"Thank you," Jax says and takes my hand to lead me across the lobby.

When we get to the elevator, I whisper, "Viscount? Expecting?"

Jax almost smiles. I see the corners of his lips come close to lifting. "A ruse that ensures my situation is managed to my expectations, and our privacy is assured." He pats my belly. "Everyone wants to protect a baby."

"You're terrible," I say, even as my stomach flips from his touch and the very *idea* of having a child with this man. I wonder what it takes to have a Vigilante vasectomy reversed.

"You haven't even begun to know how much," he says and presses the button for the top floor. It blinks, the elevator unmoving until he waves the executive key card at the pad. We begin our smooth ascent.

When the doors open, I'm frozen in place for a moment. Instead of a hallway, we're in a large atrium, sunlit from above with wide skylights. Sofas are scattered through the room and there is a bar in one corner with a silent observant bartender.

There are only four doors out of this room, two on each side. Jax takes us to the right and opens the second door.

If I thought the hotel back in St. Louis was fancy, I don't even know what to call this.

A fireplace so large you could walk into it dominates one wall. Above it is a towering painting of a girl playing a piano. There's a private bar in here too, minus the bartender, fully stocked with bottles. And a grand piano in the corner.

Like the atrium, one wall is floor-to-ceiling glass. Nashville spreads out below, colorful and bright in the late afternoon.

"It's beautiful," I say. I walk over to the piano to trail my fingers along the keys. "Do you play?"

"Rarely," he says. He walks over to the bar and pulls a bottle of champagne from a silver ice bucket. While he opens it, I notice an archway and head that direction. It leads into a dining area with the same window view. A round table is set with covered dishes and two candles, already lit. A bottle of wine is open and waiting to be poured.

"You're feeding me this time," I call out over

my shoulder. "I must have gone up a notch on your scale."

I hold on to the back of the cushioned chair. Everything in this room is a soft blue. The wallpaper. The chairs. The tablecloth. Even the dishes are white with blue trim. It's like living in a dream.

Jax comes up behind me. "Yes, a few notches," he says. He wraps his arms around me, each hand holding a sparkling flute of champagne.

I take one from him and he turns me around. It doesn't feel like afternoon now, but much later in the day. We each take a sip. It's delicious, bubbly and light, like drinking air.

Jax looks down at me, and I shiver a little. Even though we did do all those things last night, I'm still a little lost about the places we might go.

"I probably still have hay in my hair," I blurt.

Jax gives me one of those rare smiles, and I swear it's like being lit up from within. "You always say the most unexpected things," he says.

"I know. It's a curse." God, I'm so embarrassed. Why is someone like him interested in this small-town country girl?

"It's endearing." He takes my glass and sets

them both on the table. He pulls out a chair. "Let's eat something," he says. "Then we can take care of the errant hay."

My face burns hot, but I just plunk down in the chair he offers.

I peek under the silver dome. The aroma of grilled steak and creamy pasta makes me want to swoon.

Jax removes his lid and peers at the meal with suspicion.

"You don't have a poison-sensing gadget?" I ask. "I can eat first if you're worried."

Jax picks up a fork. "It's my curse," he says. "Mistrusting food."

If I'd been poisoned twice at hotels, I'd probably be the same way. "Offer still stands. I can go first."

He shakes his head. He cuts a piece of the steak, carefully watching the juice, then lifts it to his mouth

For a moment I'm mesmerized by each of his movements. The swift precise movement of the knife. The perfect angle of the fork in his hand.

I'm such a goner.

"It's delicious," he says. "You should try it."

I startle at his words. I've been staring. "Yes!" I say. "Of course."

The first bite tastes like pure heaven. I think I've been too busy or freaked out to eat anything since I met him, even during those couple of days apart. I find myself wanting to scarf it all quickly and force myself to slow down.

"Aunt Bea never cooked anything like this," I say.

He watches me with bemusement. It's the most relaxed I've seen him since that first night at the hotel in St. Louis, when he watched me with those hawk eyes.

"Tell me more about this aunt of yours," he says, his tone even. He pours the dark red wine into a glass by my plate.

A prickly sensation goes down my spine as my senses go on alert. This has always been a difficult topic. He has accused me of lying about my aunt so many times.

I swallow another creamy bit of pasta, knowing full well I won't be able to eat anymore if this conversation takes a bad turn. I take a deep breath. "She took me in when my parents died."

"A boating accident, right?"

"Yes. They were always big regatta racers. They liked going out in storms."

Jax's dark eyebrows draw together, creating his hooded look that always makes me a little afraid. "Even with you?"

"Not in storms," I say. "Although it happened." I can remember being wet and cold, the wind tossing our sailboat around. "My dad tied me to the mast once, to keep me safe. I wasn't afraid. I knew the knots." I smile at the memory.

"Sounds frightening for a child," he says.

I shake my head. "Oh, no. I felt amazingly free, tied down, so that I could stare at the storm, the crazy waves. It was exhilarating. That loss of control in the face of such unstoppable power. It's one of my favorite memories."

Jax sits back in his chair, watching me. He lifts his wine glass to his lips and just holds it there. For a moment I'm totally mesmerized by this.

"So you do have memories of them," he says.

I pick up the wine. Liquid courage. I get that now. It's heavy and strong flavored. Jax probably doesn't even know I'm only twenty and don't drink. It doesn't matter here.

"Sure," I say. "I was eight. I remember them."

"Did they ever leave you alone with a babysitter or family friend?" he asks.

I don't know where he's going with this. "Sure, to go out sometimes. I had a girl named Lori who would watch me."

"Just for evenings? Or longer?" He leans forward and sets down his glass, fully attentive.

"Just a few hours. Never overnight." I pick up my fork then set it down again. My appetite is gone. This feels like an interrogation now.

"Did one of them go away for long periods?" he continues.

I try to think, my face hot. Suddenly I get a terrible, awful feeling that everything that has happened between us was to get this information from me — even last night. What do I know about Jax? Other than he is wanted by a lot of people?

My courage flees completely, and I can't eat another bite.

"Did they?" he asks again.

"I don't remember!" I say. "Why are you asking this?"

He seems to realize he's being too harsh and sits back again. "It doesn't matter. Not now. Eat, Mia. It's good."

I can't possibly do it. My stomach is in knots. "Why do you want to know about them?"

His gaze shifts to his wine glass. He swirls the liquid easily. "I just want to know everything about you."

I don't buy it. I try to let go of my tension, but it doesn't quite ease. I make a great show of cutting off another piece of meat and sticking it in my mouth.

He reaches across the table, his fingers lightly grazing the back of my hand where I'm holding the stem of the glass. "This is our down time," he says quietly. "I won't ruin it."

My belly unfurls a little. I swallow. "What about your parents?" I ask. "Did they leave you sometimes?"

He tilts his head, as if trying to decide how to answer, then says, "Of course they did. They were Vigilantes. They had missions."

I choke and snatch up my glass, breaking his touch. Does he think my parents were Vigilantes? I gulp champagne, realize the bubbles are making me cough more, and switch to wine.

"Easy, Mia," he says.

"Is that what you think?" I sputter. "That my

parents were like you?" I shake my head. "No way. They were normal, ordinary parents. My dad worked at a bank. My mom had a part-time job as a florist."

His eyes don't let go of my gaze. I'm not sure he believes me, or if he thinks I'm deluded. But he lets it go. "And what did your aunt do?" he asks.

I frown. So we're back to that sore subject. "I don't remember her doing anything. She was always just there."

"Was she independently wealthy? Have you uncovered accounts since she died?"

My voice is small and timid. "No."

"And you never wondered how she kept up that house or paid her bills?"

"She got money for the hay," I tell him. "The neighbors used her land and gave her a cut."

"Was that enough?" Jax won't let up.

My anger starts to rise up. "She didn't need much. She didn't have a mortgage to pay. Just electric and gas and a few little things here and there."

Jax slices at his steak with more power than necessary. Somehow this makes me think of him killing someone. He said he had done that.

My anxiety peaks. I have to know who this man is.

"How did you kill him?" I blurt.

He stops, fork halfway to his mouth. "Kill who?"

"The guy. The one that got you put in jail."

He sets the fork back down. "Strangulation."

"With your bare hands?"

"With my bare hands."

I stare at those hands of his. Beautiful. Strong. I can still see them on my body, his dark fingers against my skin.

And they had killed someone.

"Why?" I ask.

He picks up his wine and takes a sip before answering, looking over the rim at me.

"Because I was under the impression at the time that he was trafficking young girls in the sex trade."

My jaw falls open. Hell, I would have killed him too.

"But you were wrong?" I ask.

"No, he was in the business. But I had no idea he was a Vigilante."

"But killing him was good, right?"

He holds his glass with both hands. "I don't

take killing someone lightly."

"How do you know who to kill and who not to kill?"

He twirls the glass, looking intently at the swirling wine. "Generally, if they are shooting at you, it's okay to kill them."

"But this guy. He wasn't shooting at you?"

"Doesn't matter. He was a Vigilante. You don't murder one of your own." Now his eyes meet mine again.

I have to clear my throat before I can squeak out, "But you're a Vigilante and they're trying to kill you now."

"That's different. I'm under a kill order." He sets down the glass without taking a sip and picks up his fork. "They're following orders."

"Does a kill order ever get canceled?" I ask, my heart hammering.

"I don't know," he says, twisting the fork in his pasta. "There's never been one for a Vigilante before."

My back is ramrod straight. My hands are in tight fists. I don't see any way for us to get out of this. How long can we go before they catch up to him?

My face burns hot. I pick up my fork, trying to quell my nerves. This is what I wanted, right? To have Jax to myself. To go with him no matter the consequences. But now my only home is in pieces. Everything I own is lost.

Suddenly I remember the stash under the pantry floor.

"Won't the fire department find all the Vigilante things?" I ask. "Won't they know something was up?"

Jax shakes his head. "It will be handled."

"Really? You guys control the fire department?"

Jax runs a finger along the top edge of his wine glass, a slow sensuous gesture. I shiver.

"Control is too strong a word, but we have a hand in most everything that matters."

"I don't see how the Vigilantes can be such a big secret," I say. I set my fork down. There's no point in trying to eat. "People have to know."

He leans forward, his blue-gray eyes intent on me. "How many unsolved mysteries are there in the world? Cold cases? How many UFO sightings? How many news articles that don't seem to quite add up?"

"L-lots," I stammer. "But usually that's because

nobody has all the facts."

He leans back and sips his wine. "Exactly. Because the Vigilantes don't allow them to have all the facts. We mete out justice in our own way. People believe in karma, that bad people will have bad things happen. The Vigilantes are those bad things. We *are* karma."

I clasp my hands in my lap. Jax seems so intense, so intimidating when he talks like this.

"Are you ever wrong?" I ask.

He shrugs. "Possibly. But we have the biggest information network in the world."

"And all these Vigilantes live double lives? Nobody knows what they really do?"

"Not all of them. Some choose to stay underground completely. Most silo employees are permanent residents."

I pick up the champagne glass idly, then drain it. The bubbly liquid slides down my throat, chilling my belly. I take in a deep breath, looking around at the room, the beautiful decor, the impeccable table, and this man.

I try to imagine living like this all the time. Anything you want, yours. Everyone around you, ready to serve. Information on anybody, puzzles to solve, crimes to figure out.

People to either rescue or punish. No checks and balances. No judges or juries.

Danger. No room for mistakes.

Still, I want it. I can't be intimidated or afraid to reach for it.

I wasn't born to this world, but it feels right for me.

I have to keep Jax close. I have to prove myself.

I think of my mother in that picture, a photo that is probably lost to me now, blown to bits.

But I keep it in my heart, her hair blowing, a reckless look in her eye. I remember, when I was small, her picking me up and telling me never to let anyone make me feel afraid. "Just because someone tries to hand you fear, doesn't mean you have to take it," she said.

I won't be afraid. And I will figure out what to do to stay with Jax, to be worthy of the work that he does. I just don't know where to start.

But then it doesn't matter, because Jax is up and coming toward me, a dark look in his eyes.

5

JAX

Even though this is a new hotel for me, I can still hear the subtle click of the door in the room next to us. Very few sounds escape me, even without enhanced hearing devices. One of the earliest Vigilante trainings centers around listening to the normal background noise of a room, and immediately detecting anything that changes.

I'm not alarmed, however. The person who has arrived is here at my request.

Mia hasn't been exposed to many things, so

what she's doing next might be new to her. But I take her hand and pull her to standing.

It isn't wise to start anything here, not with someone in the next room, but I do want her relaxed. I pull her up against me and clasp her head, my fingers running through her hair.

She sighs and rests on my chest. When her breathing has slowed and she seems past the anxiety of our conversation, I lead her out of the dining area and into the bedroom next door.

A young man is there, setting up a massage table.

Mia promptly halts. "Who is this?"

The man extends his hand. "I'm Peter. I will be administering your massage."

Mia looks up at me, eyebrows raised.

"Thought you could use it," I say, although I'm not thrilled the masseur is a man. In fact, picturing his hands on her body is starting to make me doubt this decision entirely.

He holds up a fluffy white robe. "You ready?" he asks Mia.

She takes it from him uncertainly. "Okay." She walks toward the bathroom to change.

I stare down this Peter guy.

"Viscount," he says, with a half-assed bow.

I settle in an armchair in the corner. The Peter person checks the bars beneath the table and arranges his tubes and bottles of oils.

Mia emerges from the bathroom in the robe. She looks small and timid in the piles of white terry cloth.

Peter pats the table. She's not terribly tall, so when she turns, she has to hop a little to sit on it. The robe parts to reveal her slender legs. Peter notices.

Yes, this might have been a bad idea all around.

"Just untie the front and lie down on your belly," Peter says. He unfolds a towel.

Mia does what he says, shooting me an uncertain glance.

Peter spreads the towel across her, then expertly peels the robe down so that only her back is exposed. Still, I can see the side of a compressed breast.

"Chin here," Peter says, shifting her position.

The movement causes her to lift a little, and I see more of her. I decide to escape for a moment to avail myself of the bar. We might be in Tennessee, but it's five o'clock in New York. Close enough.

40

Rather than mix my own, I head out into the shared space of the executive floor. The bartender spots me and smiles. He's an older gentleman, as they often are in these positions.

"What can I get you, Viscount Argetti, sir?" he asks.

"An Old Fashioned," I say. "Short splash. Bourbon."

He nods.

I try not to think about a naked Mia under Peter's hands as I survey the room. "Are the other suites occupied?" I ask.

"Just you here tonight," the bartender says as he expertly swirls the bitters at the bottom of the glass. "Tomorrow night, though, we have some singer. Hopefully it won't be an issue." His tone is dark.

Great. A musician.

The elevator opens directly into this room, four exits, plus the windows. The rooms are probably laid out identically, although mirrored. The bedrooms are to the inside. This hotel has eighteen floors, but none are above. Out the window and up to the roof would be the wisest escape in a pinch.

Not that I think anyone knows where we are. But positions like bartenders in posh hotels are prime locations for retired Vigilantes.

I assess this man. Sturdy, fairly fit, gray haired. I'd put him at 65. One of the telltale elements of old-school operatives is the way they always scan a room. It's something very difficult to get out of the habit of doing.

He passes me the drink, and I take a sip. "Excellent," I say.

He nods and wipes the bar.

Nope, not Vigilante. He's let several minutes go by without a visual sweep. We're in a good place for the night. I never let down my guard, but my assessment of our security ensures that I am able to focus on other, more delectable things.

I turn back to my suite and enter the spacious living room. I hear a groan from Mia and realize the bedroom door is closed.

I've crossed over to it in three seconds.

6

MIA

Jax charges into the bedroom like a mad bull.

Peter stops his magic on my tense back muscles. "Is everything all right?" he asks Jax.

Jax's eyes dart from me to Peter. I know what he's seeing. Me, no robe, on my belly, my backside barely covered by a towel. I do feel a little revealed, but whoa. Totally worth it.

"He has this oil," I begin, but Jax's glare stops me.

"We're done here," Jax says.

"But we've only —" Peter begins.

"We're done here," Jax repeats, and the menace in his voice would make a military commander quake.

It definitely makes me quiver. I hope he never gets that angry at me.

Although, I guess he probably has.

Peter snaps his bag of massage oils shut. "I'll come back for the table later," he says, shooting an angry look at Jax.

I'm amused that there's someone in the world who isn't subservient to him.

Jax's dark eyes follow him out the door. He waits until Peter has completely left the suite, then he takes a sip of his drink.

"How was it?" he asks casually.

Good grief. As if he hasn't just thrown the man out! When it was his idea!

I prop up on one elbow, knowing full well that I'm exposing parts to Jax. I'm going to make him suffer for being a possessive ass.

"Great, until some crazy man ran in here and stopped the whole thing."

His eyes are on my body. I decide to mess with him even more. I sit up, letting the towel fall behind me. I don't have a stitch on.

I see his jaw tighten. To make it a little worse on him, I dangle my legs on either side of the table. I feel crazy and brazen, but I lean back. Now it's all right there in front of him. I wonder exactly how long he can hold out.

Jax takes another drink. His gaze is hot on me, pausing on key places. Now I feel that intense rush myself, wetness and heat and the unfurling of desire.

How long can *I* hold out?

We remain in this standoff for long, excruciating seconds. His glass empties. His eyes are dark. The blue in them is long gone, all black-gray.

Calmly, carefully, he sets his drink on a side table near the door.

And I don't see it coming.

He's at me, mouth on mine, and I'm in his arms. Before I can catch my breath, I've landed on the bed, and he's on top of me, heavy and solid. The feeling is delicious, his smooth shirt and pants against my naked skin.

He grabs my wrists and takes them both in one strong hand. He lifts them up and over my head. I'm pinned, but I want it that way. If he's going to possess me, he might as well do it right.

I sense he wants to tie me down, but he doesn't have a rope, and there are no cords on the draperies. His lips rove over mine, his mouth hot, his tongue demanding. I can scarcely breathe.

I hear a jingle and a faint hiss and realize he's removed his belt. My heart speeds up.

He breaks the kiss a moment and lets the soft end of the leather trail up my thigh. It lands for a second between my legs and I inhale sharply. Every part of me is on edge. I look up at him, knowing I want something but am too embarrassed to ask for it. I've barely even had sex with him, but already I know what takes things over the edge. A little bit of —

Thwack.

He slaps it lightly against me, and I cry out.

He knows.

I look up at him, the sting flashing through my body like an electric shock.

His eyes are on me. I remember in the barn, when I surprised him by saying, "Harder." I know based on the letters he wrote me that this makes us a fit. He can say those words were code, but I know that in order to write them to begin with, you have to know what you're talking about.

This is what he likes.

Rough then gentle. The extra burn makes the pleasure that follows all the more intense.

I get it.

I learn fast.

Thwack.

I clutch at his hand, igniting with the contact. This time he drops the belt and applies the touch after, a finger slipping inside.

Now I moan. I can't manage. I need more. I writhe beneath him, trying to make him work faster, harder. I'm heading up that peak and I want it now.

He chuckles. "Oh, it's not going to be that easy for you. Not after taunting me on the massage table."

My eyes fly open. He withdraws his hand and picks up the belt. He encircles my wrists, then weaves the end through the slats on the headboard. With a quick tug, he has me locked down, my elbows by my ears. I'm exposed again, like in the barn.

But this time I'm not the least bit afraid.

He puts his hands on my waist and neatly flips me over onto my belly.

"On your knees," he says, and guides my legs underneath me.

He comes up behind me and runs his hands down my back, then my bottom, sliding down the curve until he finds me.

"Spread your knees," he says.

I do what I'm told, so desperate, so full of need, that I'll follow any instruction.

His fingers come up inside me, one on the swollen nub. I jerk when he touches it. The contact is like a spark. Then I rotate down on his hand, wanting to work toward that climax, to let loose the tension in my belly that is driving me insane.

"Not yet," he says, and his free hand comes around me, his arm locking around my middle. He holds me up, stilling my movements. I am at his mercy.

The belt keeps me in place. There are no knots for me to untie. I keep my head down, my breathing hard and erratic. I need this more than I can bear. I never knew I would want something so dark, so much.

When I've gone quiet and still, he begins to work me again, on his terms. His fingers explore every part of me. I relax into it, letting pleasure wash over me. And I understand. I was rushing things. Pushing too fast too hard. I have to let him control it, control me.

A long moan escapes as he picks up the rhythm. He seems to trust I'm on board now and releases the tight grip on me, massaging a breast instead. He tugs at a nipple and another rush flows through my body.

His mouth is on the back of my neck. "You are so deliciously wet," he says. "I'm not going to be able to resist that."

He turns me around onto my back again. He steps away, and my whole body quakes with the loss of his pressure and his warmth.

"I know what I want," he says. He reaches beneath the pillows, and jerks the covers off the bed from underneath me. I land on a cool sheet.

He pulls that down as well and begins to wind the length of it around his hand. "Won't be able to reach these ties," he says wickedly.

His dark hair is mussed. He takes my ankle and winds the sheet around it, then lashes it to the knob at the bottom corner of the bed. His hand slides up my shin, over my knee, and along my thigh. I drop my head back, waiting for the touch I'm longing for.

But he continues, going back down and wrapping the opposite corner of the sheet around my other ankle.

He's tied me down, spread wide across the bed.

"Let's put a little more light on the subject, shall we?" he asks. He walks to the window and jerks the curtains open wide. The late afternoon sun blasts inside. The windows take up the entire side wall, floor to ceiling. We're on a high floor, so no one can see in, but I feel like I'm on display. It's hot and intoxicating. I imagine someone watching us, watching me, and another hot thrill flows through me.

Who have I become? I'm so brazen. It's like I skipped past virginity 101 and straight into my doctorate.

Jax turns to survey me. He gives a little growl and lunges for the bed. His mouth is everywhere, breast, belly, then down into the folds.

I lurch up, pressing into him. His tongue is intense, lapping at me, then he's sucking on the nub. His hand steals upward to clasp my breast and I'm losing it, shattering, the need exploding out into an orgasm.

Jax feeds it, taking it higher, extending it out.

His hands move beneath me and lift me more firmly into him. The cascades keep coming, and I'm crying and saying random words and totally totally lost.

He lets me come down, but only a little, before he works his way up my body, his mouth trailing along my skin. He takes a nipple in his mouth and he's already back, fingers inside me, keeping me going, refusing to let me rest.

I don't know that I can handle any more, the pleasure sliding over into an exquisite form of torture. I want to touch him, to lower my arms, to move my legs. But I am his, and I'm not in control here.

He breaks away and strips off his shirt. "No more seeing what I'm up to," he says, and the sleeve comes over my eyes. He ties it down and the world is reduced to shadows through the white cotton.

I hear the thud of his shoes on the floor and the cool hum of his zipper coming down. I want to see him, that hard chest and flat belly, those powerful thighs. But I can only listen and breathe.

Sensations become intense. The cut of the belt into my wrist. The coolness of the sheet around my ankles. I smell him on his shirt, aftershave and outdoors.

The room gets deadly quiet. I strain, but I can't hear anything.

Then there's a tinkle of ice, melting and falling in his glass across the room.

Or not. It seems closer than that.

I know what's coming a second before it hits. The icy shock of cold against a nipple. I buck up on the bed and jerk my head from side to side. It's torment, and just when I don't think I can take it another second, it's gone, replaced by something warm, wet. His mouth. He breathes hot against me and the relief and pleasure is so intense that I want to weep.

Jax continues to work the tortured skin until it is warm and pliant again. Then he pulls away.

Without any contact, I don't know what is next. I hold my breath, trying to fix on his position in the room.

Something warm and wet dribbles on my stomach and slides into my belly button. It pools there for a moment.

Then the smell. Spicy and fruity. The red wine.

I feel his hair tickle my skin, then the hot lapping of his tongue. When he withdraws, I shiver from the chill where he's left me damp.

Then he's at my mouth, and he tastes like the wine. We touch nowhere but our lips, and I lift into him, trying to create pressure.

But Jax is elusive and doesn't allow me even a small measure of control.

"One more thing," he whispers. "And then I'm going to take you however I want."

7

JAX

Mia keeps surprising me.

I pull away from her naked body, arms tied over her head, ankles lashed to the bedposts. The sun caresses her skin, flawless and smooth.

I can't help myself, but let my fingers travel down all the planes and curves. The swell of those luscious breasts, the tightly puckered nipples, the small bump of her ribs and the concave of her belly.

I take a firm grip on both hips, squeezing. She's spread wide, open for me. Just to torture her, I lean down and run my tongue along those tender exposed parts of her. They are mine, and even my jaded self revels in the fact that they have only been mine.

She seems none the worse for wear for having lost her virginity the night before. Her pain threshold is high, perhaps. Maybe that's why she likes what she does. It bodes well for a Vigilante to withstand anything. And for Mia, maybe even to like it a little.

My erection jumps at just the thought of it. I've unleashed every brutal instinct I've ever suppressed in the name of being a gentleman on this girl, and she wants more. I keep waiting for her to tell me to stop, to show any sign that I should go back to something more traditional, more vanilla, as they say.

But she doesn't. Danger is in her blood.

She's utterly still. Listening.

I won't give her a hint of what's to come. Watching her glisten up with every new sensation is my obsession.

This one last thing will require a bit of preparation. I have nothing on hand that is designed for what I'm about to do, but Vigilantes know how to craft a tool from whatever materials might be available. I can be resourceful.

I snatch up one of the pillows. As expected, they are high quality and filled with feathers. I rip open the end. Mia startles a little at the sound.

The feathers are light and soft. Perfect. She'll think it's a break from the more intense striking play, like with the belt. But she'll be wrong.

I jerk a tissue from a container next to the bed. I roll it in a line. To make the feathers behave, I grab a handful and dunk the tips in the watery remains of the Old Fashioned. The wet ends are much easier to tie together in a tight clump, like a feather duster. I knot them securely with the rolled-up tissue.

I touch it to the tender spot under her chin.

Her concerned expression softens when she feels it.

"Ahhh," she says, opening her neck to the sensation.

She doesn't seem to realize that there is not much that is more difficult to manage than a prolonged tickle.

I drift down, encircling her breasts. She writhes a little, enjoying the soft caress.

I dip it into her belly button. She smiles, almost giggling.

I stay there a little longer, knowing we're going from a tickle to a forceful irritation. Mia's movements begin to become more forceful, trying to shift the prickle to new areas.

It's getting to her.

"Jax," she says. She's still in the realm of normal sensation, unable to push past it. So far she's enjoyed the short painful strikes of flogger or belt, but this is a whole new level. I will push her, just to see if I can take her into that euphoric space where pain and pleasure cross back and forth over the same threshold.

I shift down, just below her belly, but not any farther. For a moment, she is still and patient, but then she begins to squirm again.

Her breathing speeds up. She's trying to manage it. I drop down, hitting her squarely where she is most sensitive.

At first she moans, enjoying the attention to those delicate parts. But then she's struggling against her bonds, arms thrashing.

"I can't take it," she says. "I can't do it." Her voice is strained.

I know she's close to the end of her tolerance. I go a little longer, just a hair more.

She lets out a low groan.

I jerk away the feathers and smack her hard with my palm.

She jerks up, everything quivering. Her whole body tenses and she cries out, her words unintelligible. I press my hand hard against her, feeling the shudders come over her.

"Oh God, oh God, oh God," she keeps going on. I stay in place, holding firmly to her, feeling her orgasm ripple out. Then I can take it no longer myself.

I kneel between those soft thighs and thrust into her in one hard move.

Mia lurches up against me, and I wonder if I am too rough for her so soon after last night. But then I have to laugh because she's got her hands on me, pushing me in. She's figured out how to get out of the belt and I haven't even noticed.

I pull the sleeve away from her eyes. "You amaze me, Mia Morrow," I tell her.

"Show me how much," she says.

I hold on to her hips and move in a steady, hard rhythm. Her breasts sway with every movement and I can't look away. Everything about her is perfect, delectable. And mine.

She sits up, holding on to me, bending her knees now so that she can move with me even with her ankles tied.

I'm not sure who's in control anymore now, as I'm getting lost in the feel of her breasts against my chest.

My body moves within her, steadily, with increasing frenzy. Her breathing speeds up, and I can tell when this deeper, stronger orgasm begins because a low moan comes from her throat.

I concentrate on taking her where I want her to go. Then, unexpectedly, she moves her head and bites me on the shoulder. Hard.

Shit. That's it, I unleash inside her. She shudders around me, and the room echoes with both of us going over the top. Her arms clutch at me, and I hold her tightly. We're breathing at exactly the same rate, chests rising and falling in tandem.

We don't move for a moment, caught in that airless space of the aftermath.

Then she draws in a breath. "Jesus, Jax," she whispers. "You're going to ruin me for any other man."

And I realize then, she's ruining me too.

8

MIA

Mind. Blown.

I try to pull myself together as Jax unties my ankles. "This was in one of the letters, wasn't it?" I manage to say. "The ankles? The tickler?"

His hand rubs my skin where the sheet has left an imprint. "I believe it was, yes."

"So you knew me before I knew myself."

He laughs. "I knew for damn sure you weren't Klaus."

I fall back on the bed.

"We're going for him, aren't we?"

"Yes."

"Do we have to? Can't we just keep living like this?" I look at him. "Or are you poor now that the Vigilantes are trying to blow you up?"

I think he will chuckle, but he answers very soberly. "I would never put my finances in the reach of my employer," he says.

He slides next to me, his head propped up on his hand. He trails a finger along my ribs, and I shiver. "Besides, do I seem poor?"

"No." I have no idea what it costs to stay in a place like this, having people believe you are royalty, and waiting on your every whim. "Is it worth going after Klaus?"

Jax falls onto his back, his hands behind his head. I already miss his touch on me. I turn in to him and place my head on his shoulder. His skin is golden and smooth. He must have some Italian in him. Makes sense. De Luca. Plus, he's going by Argetti now. It definitely works for him.

His voice is low, a touch of bitterness giving his words an edge. "I've had everything I've worked for all my life snatched from me over one incident. I'm going to locate Jovana and Klaus, and I'm going to

61

find out what the hell they're involved in."

A huge lump forms in my throat and I can barely swallow around it. "I'm with you," I say. "I can honestly say that I don't care if I go down with you. As long as I'm with you."

"Dying is on the table," he says.

"I know it."

He turns his face to me. "There aren't many people like you in the world," he says.

I shrug. "I guess people like us find each other, then."

He moves his arm around me and draws me firmly against him. This was what I wanted. What I hoped for. For him to acknowledge me. To show me a sign that he gets that we're a fit.

And I meant what I said. There's nobody out there who will miss me. Nothing behind me is worth staying back for. Everything that might happen to me is out ahead.

I'm not going to be too scared to run toward it.

"When we get to the arena, I'm going to be looking for the two of them," he says. "My aim is to get them to meet me somewhere less public. They probably know by now we're not dead. I'm sure Vigilantes combed the wreckage of your house and know we got away."

I picture strangers going through my home and shudder.

He squeezes me. "Judging from the last time Jovana went to a public MMA match to watch her brother, Klaus is against her being there. That makes them at odds with each other. We can divide and conquer. Klaus isn't going to like you, because you already bested him once." At that, I can feel Jax's cheeks move into a smile. I turn my head to see it, but by the time I've moved, his face is serious again.

He looks down at me. "He isn't going to be pleased to see you again."

"Good," I say, remembering his icky touch on me. "I'm already upset I didn't kick him in the balls."

"You might get your chance," he says. "Because you're a special, they might treat you carefully. But they might know why you're special. And we don't."

"How can we find that out?" I ask.

"Normally when records are wiped, even someone like Sutherland, who is in charge of the entire operation, can't access them."

"Someone must be able to."

"Only the oversight committee can empower someone to open a record like that."

"But electronic records can be hacked by anybody," I argue.

He shakes his head. The sun is setting through the windows now, and the gold light warms our entwined bodies. "These records aren't on the grid. They are on a single off-network, air-gapped machine, guarded like it could destroy the world."

"Really? Something about me could destroy the world?"

His blue-gray eyes search mine. "Maybe. But more likely you are being protected. No telling why. It's not something I come across very often."

"Huh." I snuggle into his chest. Only after we've been quiet a while, the sun's glow shifting to red, do I realize something important.

Jax is telling me his plans. We're going to do this thing *together*.

9

JAX

The arena is smaller than the ones in Vegas I'd been to back in my Vigilante days. The fighter culture was huge, but here it seems people don't know quite what to expect as the crowd filters in and finds their seats.

Down on the floor is the octagonal fighting ring. Installed overhead are Jumbotrons that will give close-ups of the match.

Mia and I sit on the second tier near the back. It was easy enough to pick up a pair of scalper tickets, all cash and no trace of our arrival. I peer through a pair of binoculars at the crowd, scanning for Klaus or Jovana. No sign of them yet.

"Can I try those?" Mia asks. She's vibrating with excitement to be doing something other than being on the run. She bought a black "Strong Man" T-shirt without knowing a thing about the fighters and pulled it on over the silk number Armond sent. She's a country girl through and through.

She made me pick up a matching hat. Probably a good call. I don't blend in well with the locals, even though I did put on jeans.

I hand her the binoculars. "Don't push any buttons," I say. "Particularly that red one there." I point it out.

"What does it do?" she asks.

"Poison dart."

Her eyes get big. "Maybe I shouldn't." She tries to hand them back.

"No, no. We've got antidotes in the car."

She frowns, probably remembering coming out of her own poisoning after we escaped the silo. "Is there a safety or something?"

"Vigilantes don't believe in safety locks. Safe isn't what you're going for." I consider the entrances and exits while Mia fiddles with the binoculars. There are many all around the arena. I chose these seats because they would be behind wherever Jovana would likely sit, hoping to be near her brother. But not at the far back, where it is easier to be spotted.

An announcer comes out and begins talking up the fight. There will be six matches on the card. I thumb through the program. Jovana's brother, Lukov, is third.

I spot a familiar figure down low. Colt McClure. He's the one who told me about this match in our helicopter ride from Vegas. He's with another fighter I remember, Parker. His girlfriend, Maddie, is the one I helped recover after another fighter snatched her.

I should have realized Colt would show. He can't know about the altercation with the Vigilantes after I left his chopper. Although he might know that I destroyed his father's car. I should wire The Cure some money for that.

Colt scans the crowd but doesn't spot us. I've chosen our location well.

The announcer starts shouting into his microphone as the first fighter comes out of the tunnel and toward the center cage.

A giggling woman in a sparkle-laden shirt, pushup bra, and at least a gallon of drugstore perfume plops into a seat near me. She's followed by a guy in a ball cap. He looks like he may have had a beer or two in his lifetime. His gut hangs over a big silver buckle like it's a knapsack.

Mia glances over at her, sees the ten miles of cleavage on the woman, and her face contorts in a "whoa" expression. She looks at me to see if I've noticed. Ah, these relationship games. I lean over. "Switch that green dial to MMW and take a look at her," I say.

Mia looks at the binoculars and finds the control. Then, casually, she aims them at the woman. I can hear the mechanism adjusting from distant to close-up view.

She jerks them from her face. "I can see her implants!" she hisses into my ear. She looks at the binoculars again. "What is this thing?"

"Millimeter wave scanner. Been in airports since 2012."

"They can see through everything!" she says. Then she picks them up again and points them at my groin.

"I think I like this," she says and grins up at me.

Then she frowns, aiming the binoculars at her own lap. She yelps and pulls them away again. "It's like those ads in the back of comic books when my parents were young! They used to talk about them!"

"X-ray vision, yes," I say, amused. "I remember them."

Now she's all curiosity, scanning around the arena. The first fighter strips off his sweats and enters the octagon in his fighting shorts.

"I think he does steroids," she says, and I have to cough into my hand to keep from laughing.

She hands them over to me. "You should get back to business," she says, then takes them back and switches them out of MMW mode. "Okay, now."

My lips twitch as I'm about to smile again. This girl is going to ruin my reputation as a menacing man.

The lights suddenly dim and the music increases to ear-thumping levels.

"And now it's our homeboy, Jason 'The Meatgrinder' Jamison!" the announcer shouts over the din.

Spotlights crisscross and focus on the boy, early

twenties at best, as he heads up to the cage. I scan the seats ringing the stage. Colt and Parker stand and clap for him. There's still a number of empty seats down low.

Maybe she won't come until Lukov's match.

I settle back in my seat. Might as well just watch the show.

The ref brings the boys together and says something unintelligible, just a mumble of reverberating speaker noise. I glance over at Mia, who is rapt, sitting forward in her seat. Color washes over her as the lights pulse and move around.

This feels so normal, so civilian, sitting in an arena attending a public event with a crowd. Beer guts, pushup bras, and all. I shift in my seat. It's almost like she said last night, forgetting about the vendetta and Klaus and just living a life.

I have more than enough money to last ten lifetimes, no matter what I do. We could do anything.

She looks over at me and pats my leg. I take her hand and bring it to my lips. I can't see her blush, but I know it's happening by the way she casts her eyes down.

Pushup-bra woman leans over the empty seat between us. "He's a keeper," she says to Mia.

I've been exposed to a lot of toxins in my career, but her overdose of cheap perfume makes my head rush. Mia catches it too, as she absently brushes her hand across her nose.

"I think so," she says to the woman, or shouts it, rather, as the music has gotten crazy again now that the ref has stepped back.

A buzzer sounds and the two men begin their patterns. One slams a hard kick into the other and the crowd roars in appreciation.

I watch Mia's reaction. I'm curious to see how she feels about violence, if she's a shrinking violet who will look away.

But she's up, out of her seat, jumping up and shouting, "Kick him again!" The crowd all gets to their feet as the action in the cage gets more aggressive, the two men tearing after each other.

Mia can't stand still, hands in the air, yelling in chorus with all the voices around us.

No shrinking violet here, for sure.

The flying arms and legs slow down when one fighter gets the other in a submission hold, elbow locked around his neck, one leg wrapped around the other guy's. They fall to the floor.

Then suddenly the ref is on the ground, looking intently, and one of the guys jumps up, arms in the air.

"What happened?" Mia asks. "I don't get it."

"The other one tapped out," I say. "Submitted."

I scan the arena one more time. Still no Jovana or Klaus. With the unexpected lengths of these matches, some ending in less than a minute, like this one, she should be here.

She must have bowed to the pressure not to come, not with everything going on. She did, after all, try to kill us just yesterday.

If they don't show, I'll have to decide on a second plan.

10

MIA

This is the coolest thing I've ever been to.

The second fight goes longer than the first. These guys are super tiny, flyweights, the announcer says. The program says they only weigh 125 pounds, and that seems crazy. They zip around like acrobats, tossing each other into the cage walls.

Jax seems disappointed that Klaus isn't here. I know I'm not much help, but I do try to keep him distracted. When the model-perfect ring girl comes out to hold up a big card announcing the start of the next round, I make a big show of moving the dial on his binoculars to MMW and wiggling my eyebrows.

I don't know what we'll do next. Judging by the concentrating scowl on Jax's face as we approach the third match, he's plotting something.

The brother of this woman he knew, Lukov, is devastatingly handsome. I take the binoculars again, forgetting they are in see-through-clothes mode, and focus in.

Oops. I can see every muscle. Each bulge.

Yes. Each. Bulge. He's definitely *not* on steroids.

I pull the binoculars down sheepishly and switch the modes. But Jax isn't paying any attention. He's scanning the people who follow Lukov in. A trainer. Some boy who holds his towel. A couple others. But no women. And not the woman he's looking for, it seems.

I'm not sure if I'm disappointed or relieved. This woman was Jax's lover. He apparently cared enough for her to kill a man because she asked him to. That's no small request. I can't possibly imagine requesting something like that.

If she is as beautiful as her brother is gorgeous, I'm going to feel very outclassed. Not that the feeling isn't something I'm used to. It's just that lately I've been more brave. Not trying to disappear into the wallpaper.

Jax takes the binoculars from me and peers intently through them. I can feel the tension in his body, coiled, like a hungry lion. The thought makes heat rush through me. I like him this way. Intense. Professional. Sharp.

The sweet guy taking my hand a minute ago was nice. But this is an entirely different set of muscles contracting.

I want to fan myself.

The match begins. Lukov and his competitor, Growler, are evenly skilled. I keep my cheerleading reined in, although I have to resist shadowboxing as they hit each other in the ring.

The match goes through all three rounds. The judges declare Lukov the winner. When they leave the ring for the next match to start, Jax stands up. "Let's go," he says.

I follow him past the cleavage woman and her husband and out the back entrance. Then we're in the lobby area.

"What are we going to do now?" I ask.

Jax shoves the binoculars into a knapsack.

"Follow Lukov. This is a big win for him, and Jovana is bound to call to congratulate him. She might still be in town. She could be in some disguise I can't spot."

"Don't you have one of those heat signature thingies?" I ask. Vigilantes always seem to be able to identify people in strange ways.

His voice is bitter. "She's a special. She won't show." He starts striding rapidly toward the exits. "I want to be out back when Lukov comes out."

"You don't think he'll stay for the other matches?"

"No. I know the drill from my Vegas days. He'll have some media interviews, then an after-party. I'm betting if Jovana's in town, she'll come to that."

The air is cool as we burst through the doors and into the night. It's quiet with the matches still going on. Only a lone security guard leans against a pillar, smoking a cigarette.

"How will we find out where the party is?" I ask.

He doesn't answer for a minute. When we've walked a solid block from the arena, he finally says, "I have some fighter friends. I'll ask them."

We've parked the Aston Martin a good half mile away to make sure Jovana and Klaus don't spot it, but we pass the turn to the lot where it is stashed.

"Where are we going now?" I ask. I don't believe for a second he's forgotten where it is.

"I'm looking for a car to steal," he says.

I halt. "A what?"

"A car. I can't exactly drive the car Klaus has used for the past year right to the door."

Excitement tingles. I like the idea of stealing another car. "What are we looking for?"

"Something fast. And that looks like it's parked somewhere semi-permanently so that it won't be noticed as missing right away."

He points to a posh-looking building. "An apartment high-rise. A lot of them have standard parking for the residents. But most also have additional spots you can rent. That's where you put your play cars, the ones you don't drive often."

Jax is describing a world I have never known. Probably never would have known, except for him.

I could be dating the grocery store sacker right now, planning a small-town wedding and deciding on a charming fixer-upper to buy.

We turn down the ramp to the garage beneath

the building. It's full of normal cars and trucks. Jax heads toward the elevator. We step inside, but he just glances at the buttons and walks out again. "It'll be the underground level," he says. "It's the least convenient."

I don't ask why we take the stairs instead of the elevator. Maybe it's like his poisoned hotel food, a little quirk of Jax's.

We walk down a level. Here the cars are way fancier. Sporty red BMWs and some older classic cars. Several are under tarps. I recognize a 1965 Mustang. Jax pauses beside it. "Good for power, but I probably need a few modern amenities."

He peers beneath the cover of a shiny blue sports car. I walk around it.

"What is it?"

"A 2017 Acura NSX," he says. "I had one of these just before I got the Aston Martin. Amazing cars."

He pulls off the canvas tarp.

"It's beautiful," I say. And it is.

Jax opens his knapsack. Out comes a shiny square of cellophane. I remember it from our escape from the silo. He sticks it to the door and presses one of the icons. The door pops open.

"The nice thing about these cars," he says as the motor rumbles to life. "Keyless ignition, so once I'm in, I'm done."

He walks around and opens the door for me. "Your chariot."

I sit in the low-slung seat. The car smells like pine and leather. I know it belongs to someone else, but I can't help but want to keep it.

Jax folds up the tarp and stashes it behind the seat. His knapsack drops on top of it, but I notice that he keeps it close. I wonder what sort of weapons he's carrying in there. Might be better not to know. I picture again the guns beneath my aunt's house and shudder.

But this car is a dream. I run my hand along the center console. A large ball controls all the electronics in the center. "I feel like I'm in an airplane cockpit," I say.

"You like it."

"I do." I can't keep my hands off the car. The soft red leather. The cool chrome.

Jax reverses out of the spot. "Then we'll have to get you one."

I snap my head around. "What?"

"We can pick one up somewhere. Maybe we

can get to a city far enough from my identity that we can make the transaction."

"You don't have to do that," I say. I pull my hands back from the dash. I can't even imagine owning something like this.

Jax says nothing more. We navigate back toward the arena.

He pulls around to the back side, where there is a smaller lot. Food vendors and a couple of news vans are parked there, along with a smattering of cars and two stretch limos. A security guy waits by the entrance. Jax pulls up to him and rolls down the window.

The guard steps up and peers in. "You got a permit for this lot?"

"This car is a gift for Growler, one of the fighters," Jax says smoothly. "I was instructed to leave it in the lot as close to the back door as I could get. I understand his match just ended."

The guard whistles, stepping back to look at the car. "That's quite a gift," he says. But his face is firm. "They should have given you a permit."

"I understand," Jax says. He drops the car into reverse. "Of course, I'm not the one who will be upsetting The Cure McClure."

"This is from The Cure?" The guard looks over the car again. "That explains it. He's always doing things for those fighter boys." He points across the lot. "If you go around the side you can park right up near the back door. They'll come out of the metal one near the loading dock."

"Much obliged," Jax says and nods.

He drops the transmission back into drive and we pull through.

When the window is back up, I ask, "So is coming up with spontaneous lies part of your Vigilante training?"

"Some things just come naturally." Jax rolls to a stop in a space between a Lexus and a snack truck. We have a good view of the back door.

I frown. He's a natural liar? I wonder how many things he's said to me that weren't true.

Jax sees my face and squeezes my arm. "Only in the line of duty, Mia. And it will be called for over and over again. The longer you're with me, the more you'll see."

I nod, a chill coming over me.

Jax turns on the dash screen. "Civilian cars," he says with disdain. "At least it's not tied to me." He taps an icon. "Text message," he tells it and gives a number. A cursor indicates it is ready for dictation.

"Thanks for the ride the other night in Vegas," Jax tells it. "I'm at the fight. Would like to attend party."

He hits send.

"What ride?" I ask.

"Colt picked me up in the desert in a helicopter," he says. "I had to ditch my tech and my car."

I have a feeling there is more to this story, but I don't get a chance to ask, because a phone call comes through. Jax presses a button, and the car fills with the sound of the arena inside.

"The fight we were talking about during the ride?" Colt asks.

"That would be the one," Jax says. "Where is the party?"

"Inside the building. Probably minor security," Colt says. "I can get you in. How far is this going to go?"

"Could be bad," Jax says, and fear shoots through me.

"All right," he says. "I assume your people will clean it up?"

"I have no people," Jax says. "But I'll try to

keep it clean. Like Vegas."

I'm dying to know what they're talking about. I want to know everything Jax has ever done.

"Is the girl here?" Jax asks.

Okay, maybe not everything.

"Haven't seen her. I'll meet you in the halls. I trust you can get in the building." Colt's voice is almost lost to a cheer.

"Don't worry about me," Jax says. "I'll find you." He hangs up the call.

He pulls his phone from his pocket and touches the screen. "I'm going to sync this car with my phone," he says. "So that I'm using its identification. You can reach me using the car system. Just act like you are texting yourself and it will come to my phone."

"Got it." I am practically bouncing in my seat, then I realize what he's saying. "Wait. What do you mean use the car system?"

Jax opens his door, bathing us in pale light. "You're staying here."

"What?" He can't be planning to leave me!

"Mia, if Klaus and Jovana are there, they want us dead. You aren't trained for combat or evasion."

My shoulders drop. I'm back to being

deadweight. "So I'm useless."

"No. I need you out here, ready to drive. Like Colette does for me."

I look over the dash of the car. At least it's a normal one, something I can manage. "Okay," I say. "What do I do if they come out?"

He grimaces. "Let me get you something for protection." He turns to the back for his knapsack.

"Aren't you going to take that in?" I ask.

"No, too obvious."

"But your weapons. Your stuff!"

"I have plenty of tech on me," he says. "I'll be fine."

From the bag emerges a handle, metallic blue. Then a barrel.

"A gun?" I gasp.

Jax frowns. "It belongs to Klaus. I only carry darts. But this one has bullets, the newest kind, I'd guess, impact charges." He pops a magazine out. It's clear, exposing eight cylinders in metallic red.

"They were testing these before I went to prison," he says. "When they hit organic tissue, muscle or bone, they explode out."

I suck in a breath. "So you don't even have to aim well."

"Exactly." He sticks the magazine back in and hands the gun to me by the handle.

I don't want it. My whole belly shakes just looking at it.

"Vigilantes don't kill unless they have to," he says quietly.

I still don't take it. "Why do you only use darts?" I ask.

"Because most of the poison we use has an antidote, a take-back. A second chance." He turns the gun in his hand so that it glints in the overhead light. "There is no antidote to a bullet."

He holds the handle out again.

I take it with trembling fingers. "No safety, right?" I ask.

"No safety," he says grimly. He takes my hands and turns my fingers so they hold the gun correctly. "Squeeze here to shoot."

My throat burns. I can barely swallow. "What do I do if they come out? Shoot them?"

"Let them go," he says. "Only use this if they try to capture you. They tried to kill us before. They will again."

"How will I know who they are?"

He flips open his phone and hits a button. "This

is Jovana," he says.

I don't really want to look at the image, but I have to.

Well, hell. She's beautiful. Dark hair. Petite face. Dangerous and exotic.

"This is Klaus," he says. He brings up an image of a man with blond hair.

I frown. So this is the man who felt me up in the dark. I still haven't told Jax about that. I have a feeling I shouldn't.

"Okay, I've got it," I say.

He squeezes my shoulder. "You'll be fine. Come here." He takes the gun and places it on the floorboard. Then he pulls me against him, over the console. "I'm counting on you to be here and ready to get us out. Okay? If I come walking, scoot over and I'll drive. If I'm running, meet me so I can jump in."

I look out the window. It's a good fifty yards to the arena door. "Got it." I sound more convincing than I feel.

"Good girl," he says against my hair. He gives me a light kiss on the lips. "Don't message me unless you need to. It might be a distraction. I'll send you information on a need-to-know basis."

"Okay," I say. I open my door and come around to the driver's side.

Jax steps out and lets me take his spot.

He closes the door. For a few seconds the interior light stays on, then it fades out.

Jax tugs his hat lower on his forehead and strides toward the back door of the arena.

11

JAX

I hate leaving Mia out there alone, but I can't bring her inside.

Jovana and Klaus are both trained Vigilantes who want us dead.

I won't have that on my conscience.

They probably won't notice her in the car even if they go out to the lot.

If they are even here. This could all be for nothing.

But the prickle down my spine tells me it isn't.

I head to the back door of the arena. I'm stopped by a security guard, and when a friendly chat doesn't get me through, I drop him with a pinch to the vasal nerve. He won't be out long, but by the time he comes around, I'll be where I need to go.

The corridors are a maze between small dressing rooms and larger spaces for gatherings.

A message beeps through from Colt. I scan it quickly, passing a young woman carrying a tray. She notices me, but her look is more flirtatious than authoritative, so I move on.

Green room, the message reads.

That will be closer to the front. The halls get progressively thicker with people as I head nearer the arena doors. I blend in with groups as we pass the guards who prevent guests and low-level employees from entering the arena floor.

"There he is!" Colt spots me from up ahead. He pulls his own backstage pass off and sticks it over my head. With his face and public recognition, he doesn't need one himself.

"Let's head back," he says. "This way."

Colt and Parker make a point to gab about the fights as we walk the back halls to the green room. I follow their conversation only in the background, instead scanning the environment.

I pay the thoughtful and classy amenities little mind and focus on doors and layout. Whoever designed this place had crowd flow at the top of the list of concerns.

Easy to move around. Hard to defend.

The noise of the party crowd grows as we approach the entrance to the room. Through a set of double doors lies a decent-sized space filled with people in all manners of dress. Most hold drinks. A few carry small plates with appetizers.

A crowd at the bar keeps the two bartenders busy. A shorter line trickles past the buffet table. Opposite the doors are huge floor-to-ceiling windows looking out over the city. Nashville's lights dance beyond the glass.

I take all of this in over the course of the few seconds that pass before two men head over to us. They both wear off-the-rack suits that I'm sure they think are suave. One of them scowls beneath a felt fedora. The other has a glossy black mop with a suspiciously even hairline.

Colt groans. "Here comes the sleaze brigade," he mutters.

They bear down on us.

"Gunner!" the black-haired one cries and grabs Colt's hand, pumping it vigorously. "And Power Play!" He shakes Parker's hand as well and claps them both on the shoulders. "Strong as ever, I see! Thinking about going back in for that title again?"

"Ha, no thanks, Benny," says Colt. "I'm just a pretty face these days. Parker's the one on a hot streak."

Parker shrugs. "Finally found the right weight class."

The man laughs. It's a practiced, hollow sound. The kind you do on demand. He's not built like a fighter. A promoter or agent, then. His companion's only contribution to this exchange is a quick nod beneath the hat.

"And who is this?" The loud one turns to me, his hand out. "Benny Rand," he says.

I give Benny a polite smile and a firm but stilted handshake.

"Benny, this is Jax, an old friend of my family," says Colt.

Benny's eyes widen. "Whoa, quite the grip you have there, Jax." He gives a nervous laugh as I release him. "You a fighter, too?" His eyes study me, sizing me up like a rancher appraising a horse.

"Only for fitness," I reply.

"If you ever change your mind, look me up!" The hollow laugh returns. "I'm an agent as well as a promoter. I fight for your fights!"

The man is insufferable.

"Look, Benny," says Colt, "we know you're busy and don't want to take up too much of your time. You know where Lukov is?"

Benny's stone-faced companion finally speaks up. "Fly is running late, but he'll be here soon." The man's English is near perfect, but I detect the hint of an Eastern European accent.

"Ah, my manners!" says Benny. "Gentlemen, this is Anatol Bronowski, Lukov's handler." Benny claps him on the shoulder. "Fly's a real up-and-comer, eh, Bronowski?"

"He does well, yes." He talks out of the corner of his mouth, and between the suit and the hat and his scowl, it's like we're living inside a black-and-white film noir.

We exchange simple handshakes with Anatol. I spare him the full force of my grip. I need to keep him friendly.

"I look forward to meeting your fighter," I tell Anatol. He looks me in the eye then, and I see I have his attention. Good. "Make sure to introduce us."

Colt excuses us and we extract ourselves from the two of them. When we are away and Benny has safely engaged with someone else, Colt lets out a sigh.

"God, I hate that man," he mutters. "I had hoped Lukov's handler wasn't stuck with him, but there you go." He shrugs.

"Colt," I say, "I need you to separate them. I need to talk to Anatol alone."

Colt looks like I just asked him to hand in his man card.

"I'll do it," says Parker before Colt says anything. "I still owe you for Vegas."

"You don't owe me anything, Parker, but thank you," I say.

Parker nods.

"Now *I* owe you," mutters Colt.

Parker grins and claps his shoulder. "Yes, yes, you do. Go get me a beer as part of your penance." And then he's gone, pushing his way back toward Benny and Anatol.

"But then I have to bring it to him," says Colt. He shakes his head. "That sneaky bastard."

We head to the bar and fight our way to the front.

A cute girl behind the bar eyes Colt. She leans forward so her cleavage spills over the top of her artfully torn UFC T-shirt. "What can I getcha, fighter boy?"

"Whatever you've got that isn't pisswater," he says.

"You really are off the mat, if you're drinking beer," I say.

Colt shrugs. "We mostly hold them for show. Part of the gig."

"How about you, darling?" the girl asks me.

I glance at their liquor selection. I'm tempted to skip the whole thing based on the labels, but like Colt says, it's part of the show. "Mix me an Old Fashioned," I say.

She winks at me. "Classy."

We look over the crowd as she works. The room is getting packed. I'll definitely want a quieter space for what I'm here for.

"What's the plan, boss?" Colt asks.

"To keep you guys out of it."

The girl sets the drinks on the bar. "Hope you two will stick close by," she says. "I could use the company."

"We'll try to come back around," Colt says kindly and picks up his beers.

I take a sip of mine and grimace at the taste of cheap alcohol mixed in poor ratios. The downside of an open bar and a bartender who may not have been hired for her skills.

We mingle for a few minutes, chatting up other guests while keeping an eye on Parker, Benny, and Anatol. At one point Parker catches our eye and shoots Colt a pointed look at the extra beer.

"I guess I can't put this off any longer," Colt sighs. "Be quick, I don't know how long we can keep Benny occupied before either of us punches him."

Colt heads off like a dead man walking. I circle through the crowd, placing myself near Anatol without catching Benny's eye.

A woman with bottle-blond hair, poured into a sparkling black dress tries to engage me in conversation. From her speech and mannerisms, she's obviously a small-town girl. Like Mia.

Mia. God, they better not get to her. I'll kill them.

The girl pushes on my arm. "So what do you

say? Is your answer, 'Yes?'"

Hell, I haven't been listening. Mia on the brain.

And elsewhere, I think, feeling that familiar tug in my groin.

The girl finally gives up, rolling her eyes and walking off. I turn just in time to see Colt and Parker leading Benny away from Anatol.

"Mr. Bronowski!" I call before someone else distracts him. "Anatol!"

Anatol turns to me and his face relaxes with recognition. "Ah, the newcomer. Get separated from your friends?"

"I didn't want to intrude on their conversation with Benny," I reply. "Besides, I was hoping to talk with you."

"Yes, I recall, Mr.... I didn't catch your last name."

"De Luca," I say. "Jax De Luca. How is Lukov doing?"

"His win-loss record speaks for itself," he says.

I guide him to a quieter corner of the room. I pepper him with quick questions, playing up the fan angle while moving the conversation away from Lukov and toward his entourage.

"He has a sister, doesn't he?" I finally ask.

"Jovana? Yes, sweet girl. Very devoted to Fly," he replies.

I hide my bristling at the description of Jovana as "sweet." Mia is sweet. Jovana is anything but. "So she's here?"

"Oh, yes! But it's hard for her now. That boyfriend of hers is very controlling." He scowls.

Klaus and Jovana. My lack of jealousy pleases me, but I don't for a second believe that Jovana has any feelings for Klaus. It would explain his turncoat actions, however.

Maybe Klaus is using her, too. Could he be working the double-agent angle? The bombs at the safe house were clearly designed to maim and kill, but Klaus would have known I could figure out that knot. And thus survive.

I need to talk to him, alone. I have to be sure.

"Will they be with Fly when he arrives?" I ask.

"Yes, probably. Why?"

"Colt and Parker would love to meet with Fly," I say. "Probably really help his publicity along."

Anatol's interest in having his boy meet fighters at the level of Gunner and Power Play is clear on his face.

So I dash his hopes with an additional

contingency. "But I'm worried about that boyfriend being along when they meet him."

"Oh?" he asks. "Why is that?"

"If he's disrespectful to Fly's sister… Jovana, was it? I worry that Colt and Parker might do something, well, rash." I nod as understanding dawns in Anatol's eyes. "They don't take kindly to such men."

"Ah, I see. Maybe I could get Benny to speak with the man."

"I was thinking you could just shuffle Fly and Jovana off to a private room. Leave the boyfriend out here. He could mingle while the boys meet Fly and his sister."

Anatol laughs, a hearty rapid-fire chuckle. "You do not know this man. He does not mingle. And I do not know if this boyfriend would agree to let Jovana be with strange men."

"Who cares what he thinks? You represent Lukov, and he wants to meet Colt and Parker, right?"

Anatol nods. "Yes, but—"

"And I bet Jovana, being a fan of fighters too, would want to meet them. That would make Fly happy, right?"

"Well, yes—"

"Then it's settled!" I smile and grip his upper arm. "You said he was controlling. Don't you want to tweak his nose a bit?"

Anatol opens his mouth, then closes it. He looks at me, and a dark smile slowly forms.

"You are right, Mr. De Luca. It is time that *idiota* learns he cannot dictate what she does." He laughs again. "You go find your friends, and I will go find my boy." He points to a small hall off to one side. "Down there is a private lounge, find us there."

"And the boyfriend?"

"You don't worry about him. Here, I am the boss." He narrows his eyes then weaves through the crowd to the exit.

I maneuver through the throng back to Colt and Parker. Benny is nowhere in sight. Colt smiles at my approach.

"Mission accomplished?" he asks.

I nod. "Anatol has arranged a private meeting with the two of you, Lukov, and his sister."

"What about her dude?" Colt says.

"Leave him to me. But don't mention me to the sister."

Parker looks like he's about to ask why, but

Colt gives a knowing nod. "You got it, Jax."

We move to one side, where a mirrored back wall provides a view of the entrance. After a few minutes of nursing drinks and jostling against the crowd, I spot Anatol enter the room, drink in hand. Lukov is right on his heels. A few steps behind the slender fighter walks a dark-haired woman.

Jovana.

Waves of emotion slam together in my head. It takes all my willpower not to rush over and strangle her right then. I have to resist a personal revenge. She is but one piece of this puzzle now.

I almost miss Klaus through the haze of rage clouding my vision. He looks different. Haunted. In the mirror I watch his eyes scan the room, and I put Colt between us before he looks our way.

I nudge Colt. "Don't turn around," I say, "but they're here. Let them get to the back room, then make your way over there."

Colt's eyes flick to the mirror. "How much time do you need?" he asks.

"I'll find you."

He nods.

In the mirror, I watch the group move through the crowd toward the back hall. Suddenly Anatol spins around and bumps into Klaus, spilling his drink down Klaus's suit coat. Klaus jumps back and curses while Anatol grabs a napkin and fusses with Klaus's coat, dabbing and wiping. Klaus pushes him away. I can see the disgust in his eyes as he looks around.

Like any good Vigilante, he suspects a trick. But Anatol's drink was thick and fruity, and he made one glorious mess of Klaus's suit. I watch Jovana intercede and speak with him, then she gestures back to the exit.

Klaus finally throws up his hands and stalks out of the room. Anatol looks very pleased with himself as he hustles Lukov and Jovana to the hall. They quickly disappear down it.

"C'mon, Power Play," says Colt. "Let's go meet some fans."

I wend my way to the exit. Klaus will be heading to a lavatory to clean up, and the closest one is just down the hall from the party room. I pause at the door and listen. No telling how many people are inside.

I push open the door. The sound of water gushing into a basin echoes against the tile. Cautiously, I peek around the corner and an arm flies at my face. My own arm instinctively meets it in a block. A hand grabs at my own, but I twist away and jump back to measure up my assailant.

"I'm disappointed in you, Jax," says Klaus. "Did you honestly think I didn't see you in there?"

"Must have been after Anatol gave you a daiquiri bath," I say. "It certainly wasn't before."

Klaus's eyes are dark with anger. His lean body is taut with tension. The faint odor of stale cigarette smoke clings to him. His coat lies piled on the counter, one sleeve under the faucet to trick the sensor and keep the water running.

"You should have stayed put, Jax," he says.

"And let you and Jovana have all the fun? Not a chance."

Klaus rocks from one foot to the other. He knows he can't take me in a straight fight. He's looking for an opening, or stalling for time until someone comes in. Maybe Jovana.

Fine by me. Two birds, one stone.

Klaus feints left, but I step right and intercept his true action. He curses and tries to hook my leg. I step aside and let his momentum help me throw him into a bathroom stall door. The impact echoes in the small space.

He comes at me again. I block his blow, then grunt in surprise as he lands a sharp kidney shot. How did I miss that? I twist and block his kick to my ribs, but in turn accept a weaker blow to my shoulder. I spin away to reassess my footing on the slick tile. My shoes are not the best for impromptu martial arts.

The edges of my vision seem fuzzy. I inhale deeply and the uptick in my heartbeat alarms me. This skirmish should barely wind me. I know my capabilities.

Something is wrong.

12

MIA

The gun rests in my lap, blue and cold.

I'm terrified of it.

The car rumbles lightly at my feet. I wish it were electric and silent instead of gas powered. I want to disappear. If anyone notices me, comes after me, then I have to use the gun.

My breathing speeds up just looking at it.

I think about what Jax said. There's no antidote to a bullet.

Why didn't he just give me a dart shooter?

I'm going to find one myself.

I turn around and reach for his knapsack.

The inside of the car is dark and I don't dare turn on the light. I hold up the bag so the lamps in the parking lot will shine on it.

There are a lot of things inside. I reach my hand in. Out comes one of those wands they seem to use a lot. They detect stuff, but I have no idea how to use one.

I reach for something else.

The dart binoculars. Now I DO know how to use those. I wonder what the range is. It might not be good. And the tiny dart might not do much. That might be why Jax didn't give it to me. It's probably hard to aim.

Gah. I need training. I'm going to make him teach me.

I feel around in the bag and my hand closes over something small and cold. I pull it out.

The onyx ring. How interesting that he brought it. I slip it on my thumb. I wonder how it ended up in my aunt's pantry stash, and why Jax found it important enough to carry with him.

It spins on my finger. I don't want to lose it, so I take it off and put it back inside the bag.

That's it. All he brought.

Gun it is, I guess. When I turn to put the knapsack back, my knee bumps against the steering wheel base.

"Engine off," the dash voice says.

What?

The car rumbles to a stop.

Shoot. I set the gun on the passenger seat and look at the controls. I can't read anything, plus the screen is off.

"Car?" I ask.

Nothing.

"Wake up?"

Still nothing.

I poke on anything I can see. Buttons, screen, the big round control in the center.

The car stays off.

Shoot. How do keyless cars turn on? I bumped something. It can't be easy to turn the car off while it's running. It must be a feature of when it's parked. I feel along the steering column. I find several buttons and press them all.

Nothing.

Great.

I lift myself off the seat and sit down again.

Nope.

Maybe I have to get out of the car and get back in.

I pull on the handle.

Locked.

Whoa. What?

I jerk on it harder.

It doesn't open.

I put the gun on the floor and crawl over to the passenger seat. That door is locked tight too. I try the windows. They don't roll down.

I'm locked in.

And the car is off.

I breathe so hard and fast that I fog up the window on my side. I wipe it with my fist. What if Jax comes out? What if he's running?

I can see more buttons low on the dash, so I push them. Everything is dead except the slow blinking red light indicating a car alarm. I keep thinking if I hit the window hard enough, that will set off the alarm, but then what would that do? It's not like that would unlock it.

I want to scream with frustration. My head feels like it's going to explode. I'm incompetent!

As the minutes pass, I force myself to calm

down. I'm behaving like a civilian. Like I'm helpless.

I'm not. I'm getting out of here.

I start looking around the interior of the car. There has to be something in here I can use to escape. *Think, Mia!*

I crawl over the console to look out the driver-side window. I can't see below it, but I spot a faint reflection of a glow. That cellophane thingy. That's what has this car on lockdown. Jax probably didn't realize he was locking me in. Of course, he probably didn't anticipate my foolishly turning the car off.

I close my eyes, remembering all the times Jax used that special key. He blew that lid off the silo hatch with it. So it has some explosive power. And he broke into this car. There weren't any keys. It runs off a code. So it can descramble those kinds of locks.

I can't reach it with the window up, so it's useless to me. I need a way out from the inside.

I struggle to think of a way. I could break a window, I guess. But the alarm would surely go off and attract attention.

I glance at the gun. Then I might have to use it.

Think, Mia, *think*.

Don't fancy cars have a valet mode? Maybe that could circumvent that code descrambler. Do something manual to pop the door.

I feel under the dash well below the steering wheel. I find a button and press it.

A faint click outside the car tells me I just opened the cover of the gas tank. Not helpful.

I find another one, and the hood pops up an inch. Great, I'm booby-trapping the car if we need a quick getaway. I'll fix it once I'm out.

The next one makes the hazard lights start blinking. I quickly shut them back off.

Then I find another small lever. I pull it.

The car chimes. The electronics come on for a second. My heart hammers like mad.

A female voice says, "Valet mode initiated."

I tentatively tug on the door handle.

It opens!

I step out onto the asphalt. I did it! I got out! On my own! I dance in a little circle. *Go, Mia. Go, Mia.*

The exit opens at the back of the arena and I drop to the ground. Shoot. Excessive celebration. Not very Vigilante.

I crawl forward, thankful for the jeans. A drop-dead-gorgeous black-haired woman comes out, walking too fast to be normal. Is it her? I can't tell in the uneven light of the parking lot.

Maybe this woman is just late for something. She heads toward the rows of cars. I close the door quietly and move to the back of a delivery truck as she passes by about four cars down. Her hair swings like a shiny curtain. She's petite but everything about her is like a panther, strong and stealthy.

It's her. I would bet on it.

And the gun is in the car.

Crap.

Something on her wrist lights up. A watch! She starts talking into it.

A Vigilante watch?

Maybe. I mean, there are ordinary watches you can talk to. They have Internet, as well as remote controls for cars and house functions. Those have been around for years.

But they're not popular accessories. Particularly not for stylish women.

This has got to be her.

I crouch down and run alongside the cars, staying as near as I dare. She stops for a second to growl into the watch. Now I can hear her loud and clear.

"He just showed up here! Jax! Klaus is taking care of him."

Shit! She said Jax!

My breathing speeds up. The menace in her voice could scare paint off a wall.

I try to think what to do. This woman looks strong, like she's trained to take people down. But she is dressed well, in a short skirt, a button-down top, and heels. I don't care how good you are, heels make you less stable and an easier mark.

"Sutherland, are you cutting me out?" she asks. "Nobody told me Jax survived the blast."

Sutherland? The creepy dude in Colette's car? The head guy? I scarcely dare to inhale, trying to listen to every word. This is the most important conversation of my life.

"All right. Fine," she says. "I'm coming to the Washington office. I can't get there until tomorrow night." She jingles her other wrist with its collection of bangles. She's agitated. "Don't avoid me like you did in Chicago," she insists and smacks the watch. The light goes out.

I glance around. She's walking again. I have to get to her before she gets to her car.

And do what? Attack her? Shit. I need Jax. I

don't know what he wants with her.

Then I remember.

She blew up my HOUSE.

Bitch.

I don't think for another minute but take off in a dead run. I'm going to enjoy watching her pretty face skid across the asphalt.

13

JAX

The corners of Klaus's lips twitch. "Feeling okay, Jax?"

I say nothing, instead making my own feint to aim a sharp blow at his diaphragm. He blocks it and tries to throw me like I did him a moment ago. It takes every effort to resist the motion and stay put.

We trade blows and blocks. I can't gain the advantage.

Finally I grab his hand, and the skin feels strange under my grip. Loose, almost like it's disconnected. I twist and yank hard. A piece tears away with a sickening sound.

Klaus smiles as he holds up his hand. He's wearing some sort of very fine, thin glove. It imitates his real skin almost perfectly.

"The latest in Vigilante tech," he says. "Prosthetic skin as weaponry. Amazing what we can do with it." His gaze locks on mine. "Like administer contact poisons in complete safety and secrecy."

Of course. That's why he's stalling, and that's why he's able to match me.

"I had hoped the bomb would do the job," he continues, sounding bored. "Apparently I miscalculated."

So he wasn't trying to let me escape. He simply had no skill.

"You're no Sam, that's for sure," I growl.

"Yes, Sam. We'll have to do something about him someday. Colette too, I suppose. Too bad, I liked them."

I blow off his threat. "And who is *we*, Klaus? More than you and Jovana?"

"More than you know, Jax."

He's relaxed now, thinking he's won. I run

through mental exercises to control my breathing and heart rate. If he keeps talking, I may just pull this off, even with poison coursing through my bloodstream.

"I know Sutherland's involved," I say with mock strain.

"Do you now?" Klaus looks bemused. "I bet you have no proof."

"What I know, others will know soon enough. Especially if I disappear."

Klaus laughs. "No one is surprised when someone dies on a kill order. How amateur, Jax. You really are hard up these d—"

I don't let him finish. With as much speed as I can muster, I lash out but deliberately overstep the move. Klaus moves to counter with a lazy, confident block. I twist and hook his leg, throwing him off balance. I catch a look of panic in his eyes as I slip behind him. I grip him in a headlock and my fingers dig into pressure points.

"Now talk, you son of a bitch," I hiss, "or I'll paralyze you from the neck down." My anger is palpable.

Klaus gurgles and struggles. I press harder and he yelps.

"Stop! Okay! Yes, Sutherland is involved!"

"How? What's his plan?"

"I don't know! Ow! God damn it, Jax, I'm telling the truth, I don't know! It's all Jovana's game!" He gasps, his breathing ragged. "I'm just the security guy, that's all! Covering up, cleaning up! Like always! I swear!"

Klaus never was very brave.

"Where is Sutherland now?"

"I don't know! Again, Jovana. Ask her!" He sucks in a breath. "Seriously, Jax. You don't have much time." He pauses. "You need an antidote. And Jovana has already left. We agreed that if we got separated, she would take off and alert Sutherland."

My anger cools. I can feel the poison working faster as my blood rushes. I have to stay calm, slow it down.

Klaus coughs, a weak and helpless sound. "What's it going to be, Jax? Go get your antidote or finish me off?"

I answer him with a sharp blow to the back of the head. He slumps in my arms and I dump him on the cold tile floor. Then I stagger out the door.

The antidotes are in my car. Not the one in the parking lot, but the Aston Martin a half mile away.

14

MIA

Jovana stops walking, her back to me, as if she's waiting for me to arrive.

Just as I reach her, ready to knock her to the ground, she turns.

Her arms are a blur as her fist slams into my belly, then her elbow crashes against my chin. I stumble for a minute, but I'm in a blind rage, so I launch myself at her again.

I remember how Jax brought me down with a blow to the back of the knee. I kick at her leg, miss by a mile, but in the heels she isn't quite as solid, so she takes an uncertain step to the side.

My adrenaline is surging as I wrap my arms around her waist and bring her down. We both land on the asphalt, but it's my arm that takes the brunt of the fall.

Pain screams through my body, but I ignore it. I figure if I can't beat her in a fight, I can at least make her life difficult for a little while. I snatch at the watch and jerk it from her wrist. It flies through the air and lands with a crunch somewhere down the row.

"You little bitch!" Jovana says. She's trying to get her hands on my neck, and I know what that's all about. Jax did that pinch thing to me in the car.

Not today.

I grapple with her, keeping her from getting enough control to bring me down with one of those death grips. Her bag falls off her shoulder, and I kick it like a football, scattering the contents. Might be something interesting in there if I can grab it.

She rolls me onto my belly, and I know from watching the fights that this is bad. I don't let the momentum stop, though, and manage to keep going so I'm on my side. Now her bag and its secrets are under me. I reach behind me with one hand, trying to find something to use against her, while the other fends off her attempts to get me in one of those vise grips.

I'm already wearing out, though, and I know this battle is going to end as fast as it started if I can't find a way to get the upper hand. All I've had working for me so far is the element of surprise and her high heels.

I find something round and metal and hold it out. It's a weird little device with a bottle attached. I push down on it and a vapor steams out of it.

Ha, a lethal gas, I bet. I hold my breath as Jovana blinks from the rushing of air.

She knocks it away. "What, you going to kill me with my asthma treatment?"

Damn.

She jumps on top of me, pinning my arms.

I'm screwed now. My breathing is labored, my heart crashing in my chest like a mad drummer in a punk band. She wanted me dead in my house. This might be it. The beginning and end of my Vigilante days.

"Who the hell are you?" she asks.

"Your worst nightmare," I say.

Smooth, Mia. Quote a bad movie.

Her perfect eyebrow quirks up. Even with her hair all over the place, she's undeniably one of the most beautiful women I've ever seen. It's not lost on me that she's sitting over me like she probably used to do on Jax.

I go limp on the asphalt. I've messed up in so many millions of ways. Jax is going to kill me.

If his Vigilante ex-lover doesn't first.

"What are you after? Money? Drugs?" Jovana's expression is hard. "You picked the wrong bitch to mug."

Light begins to dawn. She doesn't know who I am. Like, really doesn't. Hasn't she seen my picture?

Of course, I don't photograph well. Probably the only thing in their system is my driver's license, where I resemble a strung-out meth addict. Plus, I'd tried to give myself highlights the day before, and it looked like I had spaghetti stuck in my hair.

"You got any cocaine?" I ask. "Angel dust? PCP?" I don't know what the hell I'm saying. That's all I can remember from some anti-drug lecture in sixth grade.

Jovana pushes away in disgust. "You filthy

Americans," she says. "Your self-destructive habits." She stands up and snatches her purse. "Pick up my things."

"You got cash, then?" I ask.

"Ugh, here." She flings a wad at me. Dollars flutter against my chest and I trap them as if I'm desperate.

I shove them in my jeans pocket and pick up the items on the ground. Nothing special. Normal girl stuff. Lipstick. Mirror. Receipts. Then something. A strange silver wand. I pick it up.

Jovana snatches it from me. "Now scram," she says.

I turn away and run.

I don't look back as I dodge cars, weaving through them, my hands clenched tight. I pretend to stumble, pick myself up, and keep going. I slow down as I hear a door slam and an engine whir, the quiet whine of an electric.

She drives along the rows and leaves through the guarded exit. Only then do I stop and turn around to head back to the blue Acura. I could believe that I utterly failed in my task. If I wanted to stop her, then it's true.

But I didn't fail. She has a meeting with

Sutherland tomorrow night she can't be late for, not after her hissy fit. And I can't wait to tell Jax that I know where she's going.

And that she's missing this.

I open my fist. Her watch is in my hand.

JAX

The corridors are a fun house of people, colors, and walls that don't want to stay still.

I push through the crowd, my breathing labored, trying to focus, vainly hoping to keep my heart rate low, slow the poison down.

The halls get quieter as I near the exit, grateful I have managed to stumble the right way.

Then a voice, menacing and low. "I've been looking for you."

It's the security guard I dropped earlier. He's

rubbing his shoulder.

He looks wary as I approach. He unclips his radio from his belt and says into it, "Found the perp. Come and get him."

Whatever. I hold my arm out menacingly and he backs away. I walk past him. I've almost made it.

"Oh, no, you don't," the guard says. He comes up behind me and cracks me on the head with something.

I turn to drop him again, but he has a friend with him now.

The two of them reach out with their arms, both holding their radios like they're going to whack me again. With radios.

"You know, you're going to break those," I say. "They'll probably dock your pay."

The new guy looks up at the radio, as if realizing what I say is true. "My job isn't worth this," he says.

"You guys seem like professionals," I say. "I'm in the business myself."

"What business?" the first guy asks.

"Security," I say.

"Who for?" he demands.

I wave my arm around. I feel drunk. Which

poison feels like this? The one Mia had? I'll have to tell her which antidote to use.

The new guard steps forward, and I swing around, arms out. Their outlines are fuzzy, but I'm not out yet. "Colt McClure," I say.

"The fighter?" one asks.

"Yes, check with him. I'm fetching his car." I stab at Colt's backstage pass still hanging from my neck. "Heading out. You won't be seeing me again." I'm definitely slurring my words.

The two men look at each other.

"He has a damn pass," the new one says.

"He didn't have it before," the other argues.

I don't have time for this. "Pardon me, gentlemen," I say.

"I don't think you're up for driving," one says.

I can't distinguish them anymore. Their voices sound like they're passing through water.

I turn away and stride toward the door. "No time for chitchat," I say. They don't follow, but watch me. Their silly radios are still in the air.

I push through the exit and into the night, praying Mia is ready with the car.

The blue Acura is still in its spot and a wave of relief crosses over me. I try to run, to signal her to drive up for me before the guards come out and slow me down. But instead I'm falling, the ground rising up to meet my face.

16

MIA

Oh, no. Oh, no.

Jax. Jax. Jax!

I see him come out, stumbling, barely able to stand. Then he drops to the ground.

He's hurt!

I jerk the car into drive, glad I have it all ready to go, hood secured, fuel tank closed, and Jovana's watch tucked away in the dash.

I pull up to the arena door and jump from the car.

Jax is back on his knees, mumbling something incoherent.

Two security guards burst out the door, then halt when they see me.

I try to lift Jax, but he's too heavy.

"What are you staring at?" I snap at the two men. "Help me get him into the car."

When they just stand there, I about lose it. "Help me RIGHT NOW."

They hurry forward.

"Get the door," I tell one.

He opens it, and I start pulling Jax up to me.

"Get his other arm," I command the other.

Between us, we get Jax into the seat.

"Ma'am," one says sheepishly. "We have to take him in for attacking a guard."

I whip around. "YOU are going to take in the deputy of HOMELAND SECURITY?" I'm totally making this up, but these guys don't look too bright.

"The what?"

"He's undercover. Some of these fighters are in danger. Do you know Colt McClure? You idiots!" I throw up my hands. "I'll have you court-martialed!" As I round the front of the car, I realize they're just hired security. "Never mind. You're civilians. Just get out of our way."

They keep staring at me as I jump in the front seat. When I stomp on the gas, they leap back.

Good riddance.

As soon as we're past the exit, I gun it down the street and past the arena. There's a gas station on the next block, so I screech into the lot and slam the car into park.

I turn to Jax. "What is it, baby?" I feel along his shirt. I don't see blood anywhere. "What is it?"

He's slumped against the door.

I grab him and pull him in to me. "Tell me what it is so I can do something!" I slap his cheek.

He sucks in a breath, and I think he's going to say something, but then he slumps again.

I can't hold him. He's too heavy.

What the hell do I do? Hospital? Would the Vigilantes find out?

Oh God.

His stomach makes a strange sound, and I flash back to when I got hit by the poison dart.

Yes, that's it. He's been hit too. They got him.

Shit. How long do I have? Is the antidote in his car?

I sit back and jerk the car into gear. In seconds

I'm barreling into the lot where we left the Aston Martin.

I pull up next to it and jump out of the Acura. Jax's car is locked tight.

His watch will open it. I wrench the passenger door open and pull on his arm. Not close enough. I yank the watch from his wrist. When I whirl around, the car unlocks.

Thank God. A quick glance in the car tells me nothing useful is inside. Please tell me he didn't leave them back at the hotel. It's too far.

I punch a button on the dash, glad I got familiar with the car when I stole it from Klaus, and the trunk pops open. In the back are the Vigilante cases, both Jax's and the ones that were there from Klaus.

I don't really know what I'm looking for, but hopefully the antidotes will be in vials or tubes or needles and not some fancy method of delivery that I don't recognize. I dump out the first case. Several real guns. Those belong to Klaus. If he poisoned him, he should have the antidote.

A smaller case slides out. I jerk it open.

Five vials with capped needles.

Antidotes? Or poisons themselves?

I have no idea.

God.

I glance over at Jax. Should I hit him with them all?

That could be worse!

I need help. Must have help.

I go back to Jax and slap him again. "You have to tell me what the antidote is!"

He doesn't open his eyes.

I feel his pulse. Still there. Slow, though. Too slow. God.

I jump in the Aston Martin. The car engine whirs on and the dash lights up.

"Call Sam the Vigilante," I say.

"Mia Morrow is not authorized for that information," the voice says.

"But Jax is with me! I used his watch to unlock the door!"

"Command not understood," the voice answers. "Please try another command."

"Jax wants to call Sam the Vigilante," I say.

"Mia Morrow is not authorized for that information," the voice repeats.

I bang my hand on the dash. How do I do this?

His phone.

I jump back to the Acura and rummage through

Jax's pockets. I pull out the phone, frantically activating the screen. The contacts are empty other than the number for Colt. Colt can't help now.

The phone is still tied to the car. I run around and shut off the Acura, praying that when it's switched off, it will revert to Jax's normal mode.

As soon as the engine is down, I pull up the phone again.

Yes, the contacts are restored.

But as I scroll through them looking for Sam, I realize they are coded. Shit. I don't know who anybody is. They're all numbers.

I go to the most recent calls. Who are the people on this list?

I choose the day he left me with Colette and pick a number around that time. Whoever he would have called that day should be safe.

I punch the number and hold my breath. Please be Sam or Colette. Please. Please. Please.

Sam's voice floods me with relief.

"Jax, this is bad, you just called on an open line," he says.

"It's Mia," I say quickly. "I'm sorry. Jax has been poisoned and I don't know what to do."

"Switch to video," he says.

I find the icon and punch it.

"Show him to me," Sam says.

I turn the phone around.

"Did he throw up?" he asks.

"No," I say.

"Spasms?"

"No."

Sam's voice is calm. "See if his eyes are dilated. If the pupils are huge."

I reach down and carefully tug his eyelids apart. "Yes, I think so." I hold the camera up.

"This is important," Sam says. "If you choose the wrong one, he dies."

I open his lids again.

"Compare them to your own in this light," he instructs.

I pull back and stare into the side door mirror. "His are definitely bigger."

"I can't see well enough, but I trust you," Sam says. "Did you find the vials in the trunk of the car?"

"Yes," I say.

"Okay. Get the green one."

I run to the trunk and jerk the green vial from the case.

"Where do I stick it?" I ask Sam.

"Anywhere works, but if you can get him in the arm close to his heart, that's best."

I jerk up the sleeve to his white linen shirt and expose the crook of his elbow. That's where nurses always stick you to take blood. It must be good. I uncap the needle.

"Just let it go in slow and steady," Sam says.

I prick his skin and push the plunger in.

"Mia," Sam says. His voice is strained. "You have to get off this phone call and leave there immediately. We're all in trouble now."

"Okay. Thank you." I kill the call and throw the phone across the parking lot. It lands in a thorny bush. Maybe that will slow them down since they can track it.

I turn back to Jax. I want to take his car so we can be cloaked, but I can't move him. He's starting to stir.

I lean in. "Jax, baby, if you want to take your car, you have to move. The Vigilantes know where we are."

He opens his eyes. He shakes his head, then suddenly he's all action. He reaches behind the seat and grabs his knapsack. He pauses a moment, staring at the floorboard, and picks up Klaus's metallic blue gun.

I back away as he lunges for his car as if he's going to drive.

"Oh, no," I say. "You have to sit in the passenger seat." I grab his arm. He jerks away, then shakes his head again. I know what he's going through. I remember this manic phase. I wonder if I should take the gun away.

I walk him around and open the door. "In," I order, and he obeys.

Then I race around the car and jump in.

I don't want to go back toward the arena. That seems the most likely place they'll come from.

"Cloaking levels one, two, and three," I tell the car as we bounce over a curb and onto a dark back street.

"Cloaking initiated," the woman says.

"Look at you," Jax says. "Like you were born to it."

I flash him a smile. "You got a Crybaby in this one?" I ask.

He shakes his head, his hand on his temple. "Just drive away. They can't track us unless they get a visual. Blend into traffic as soon as you can."

I bump along the back road, scanning ahead for a busier street. We zigzag through the neighborhood, then I spot a traffic light. That should intersect with something else.

"Is it safe to go back to the hotel?" I ask him.

"Should be, as long as we're not followed." He scans the road ahead, then turns and looks behind. "We seem clear."

I look over at him and he meets my eyes. "You were great back there," he says.

I'm coming down from the horrifying adrenaline rush. "What happened?"

Jax ruffles his hair. "Klaus poisoned me. Slick new device embedded in prosthetic skin."

I grimace. "Sounds disgusting."

"It got me."

"Do you have people trying to kill you all the time?" I ask.

He holds the gun in his hand for a moment longer, letting it glint in the passing streetlights, then drops it into his knapsack. As we merge into traffic, he says, "Only once or twice a day."

17

JAX

Probably the only thing worse than dying from a Vigilante poison is surviving it.

I always imagine that this is what college kids feel like after a night of cheap liquor. Head pounding. Stomach like a punch to the gut. I don't appreciate feeling weak or slow.

And Jovana got away. Klaus has admitted to a bigger plot, but for what? I don't have a next step other than to go for Sutherland himself.

Which is suicide.

Mia drives the car with alert attention. The lights passing by light up her face and hair, then she falls into darkness again. She glances at me every few seconds as if to make sure I'm really still alive.

"I'm not easy to kill," I assure her.

"Good thing," she says. "Because you're pushing your luck lately."

Damn, she's fun. And clever. And capable.

"So what happened to you?" I ask.

"Not much," she says. "Got trapped in the car. Escaped. Played with firearms." She keeps her eyes on the road. "Oh, and jumped your ex-girlfriend."

"What?" The sound comes out like an explosion.

She doesn't flinch, expecting my reaction. Her laugh is musical and light. "She thought I was a crack whore."

"She didn't recognize you?"

"No." She reaches into a pocket and pulls out a wad of cash. "She even contributed to my habit."

"That's…odd."

"I let her think it. But I did get some information." She glances at me slyly, pleased with herself. "She's meeting Sutherland in the Washington office tomorrow evening. She was pretty pissed that you were alive. Apparently she didn't know."

"Interesting." So they aren't keeping her in the loop anymore. That's a promising turn.

"So are we going to Washington?" she asks. She seems almost afraid to ask the question.

"You're doing better than I am," I quip. "Maybe I should send you in after them."

"Well, I am a special," she says. "And we're even now on assassination attempts."

"That we are."

We've crossed a pretty solid section of Nashville now. "I think it's safe to double back to the hotel," I tell her.

"I have no idea where I am," she says with a laugh. "Should I use the car navigation?"

"Let's be old school for now, just in case," I say. I'm not so naive as to think they can't track every car that left the arena. But it's unlikely they'll get it right. We've switched cars, gone cloaked. I press my hand to my empty pocket. "Where is my phone?"

"Oh, that," she says. "Sam said it was compromised, so I tossed it."

Hopefully he'll wipe it remotely, if he can. "It

was smart to call him like that."

"And not easy." Her voice is hard. "This mean car never lets me connect to anybody."

"Voice recognition," I say. "It's a good system, mostly. You did well."

She smiles at the compliment. "So, Mr. Jax the Vigilante, what are we going to do tonight? Head on to Washington?" She tilts her head.

"Turn left up here," I tell her. "I think another night at the hotel is in order."

She bites her lip as she maneuvers the car. My body starts to right itself, my head clearing.

We'll buy ourselves one more easy night. Then back into the fray we go.

18

MIA

We're no more in the room than Jax falls back on the bed. "I think the poisons are getting more intense," he says. "Even if they save you, they want you to suffer."

I can agree about that. I find it amusing that we have this in common, being struck down by the Vigilantes. Well, funny other than the part where we were, in fact, poisoned.

Everything in the room is immaculate, our clothes clean and folded or hanging. I rummage through the suitcases Armond sent to us, looking for something to sleep in. I find a midnight-blue baby-doll negligee and take it out with trepidation.

Jax perks up at this. "Don't plan to wear that for long."

I clutch the bit of lace to my chest. "Should I bother?"

He tucks his hands behind his head. "Definitely."

I toss it at him. "You're feeling better," I say.

He lets it hit his face. "Mmmm," he says. "It smells nice." He shakes his head and lets it fall. "It will smell better on you."

This makes me flush. This sort of banter isn't something I'm used to yet. The vast gap between his experience and mine feels like an ocean.

And then there was my altercation with Jovana. She is his most recent ex-lover, even if it has been a year.

A forced year.

I sit on the bed next to him. "It was a little strange, meeting this Jovana woman," I admit.

He turns to me, leaning on his elbow. "Did you get a good blow in? To defend my honor?"

I laugh. "If only. But I did kick the hell out of

her fancy purse."

Jax growls and wraps an arm around my waist. "Come here, my sweet little badass." He drags me down to the bed.

I stare up at him. He seems none the worse for wear for having been poisoned an hour ago. But then, I guess, an hour after I was poisoned, we were in the barn, I was naked, and his hands were…

About where they're going now.

His fingers slide up my rib cage. I let out a long, slow breath for the first time since Jax stumbled out that back door and crashed into the concrete. I realize that he's meaning a lot to me. I think back to the last days in my aunt's house, pining for him. And I had no idea what was to come.

Everything has been even better than I could have imagined. I had no clue.

His blue-gray eyes fix on mine. "Tell me about your fear of guns."

I go still. I didn't anticipate this. "I just have this strong reaction to them," I say.

"Your aunt didn't have any around?" Even as he asks this, his hand trails along my spine, sending a tingle up my body.

"Not that I knew about." I hesitate. He probably

knows about the ones in the stash. "But I found the case of them under the floor in the pantry."

"When you destroyed the floor." His face shows a trace of amusement.

"Once I figured out that the shoes would open the trapdoor."

"Clever."

"I wasn't going to get it open any other way. I tried hacking it."

"Is that when you found the ring? I was surprised to find you brought it with you when you escaped Klaus."

"Yes," I say. "Something about it made me keep it."

He moves away from me, and I wish I hadn't asked, my body aching for him to touch me again.

Jax goes to the knapsack that he dropped on a chair when we came in. He pulls out the black oval ring. "It's an odd thing to have in a safe house."

"It doesn't do anything, as far as I can tell," I say. "I guess you saw it that first night?" I shiver a little, thinking about waking up to Jax at the end of my bed. I knew, even then, that something incredible was happening.

Jax sits on the bed, holding the ring in his palm.

"I think it's just a plain ring. It doesn't set off any sensors on any equipment. It looks old."

I take it from him and slide it on my thumb. "I wonder how it ended up in our stash."

"No telling," Jax says. "You seem to like it."

"I do." I take it off and turn it over. Inside, the initials KHS are engraved. "I wonder whose initials these are," I say.

"No telling. There are no Vigilantes that match them. I checked."

"Really? You were that curious?"

His eyes watch me steadily. "I was trying to find out the secrets of your safe house."

I pick up his hand and slide the ring on his finger. "It's a good fit for you."

He holds it out like a woman examining a diamond, and I burst into giggles.

"Does it make my fingers look fat?" he asks.

God, I'm dying. Jax? Playful? It didn't seem possible any time before.

I snatch up the blue negligee. "I guess I should put this on," I say.

The air seems to crackle between us. "I'd say definitely, yes," he agrees.

I pick it up and head into the bathroom.

I close the door and lean against it. My stomach is turning somersaults. I'm so lost. I want him by me all the time.

I've totally fallen for this man.

And yet, we're in so much danger. I don't see how we can get out of this. The Vigilantes seem at our heels every moment. So many close calls. Poisons. Bombs.

I turn to the giant mirrors surrounded with movie-star bulbs, like I'm in a dressing room at a film studio. I peel off the MMA T-shirt and jeans.

My hair falls in soft waves on my shoulders, probably due to the fancy shampoo and conditioner Armond sent. My life is such a strange seesaw of fairy tale and horror flick.

Probably there is a matching bottom to this filmy top somewhere in the suitcases, but it's too late to go looking for it now. Thankfully my underwear is also blue, so it works all right with the negligee.

I take off my bra, feeling sort of in awe that Armond nailed the fit on that, and tug the top over my head. It flutters down like a wedding veil, and about as transparent. This outfit hides nothing at all.

I take a deep breath and put my hand on the

doorknob. I wonder what Jax is thinking of this time. Ropes? The tickler? Something new? I feel a rush of heat just thinking about it. I don't know how I fell into the hands of a man like Jax De Luca, but I am so grateful that I did.

I open the door, trying not to feel shy in the outfit.

Jax looks up, his eyes appreciative on my body.

He's naked on the bed, his skin glowing in the soft light.

And in his lap, he holds a gun.

19

JAX

Mia takes a step back into the bathroom when she sees the gun.

I wait for her to ask about it, although I have to stifle a visible reaction to her appearance in that sheer bit of fabric. I've seen Mia in a lot of states of dress, ripped nightgown, naked in ropes in a field, and wearing a red thong and nothing else in a barn.

But this?

She's like the completion of a picture. The gold

doorframe surrounds her in the blue negligee. The room is exquisite and formal, and she fits it as though it was all put here just for her.

The curve of her breasts is outlined by the sheer blue. I want to toss the gun and just take her, but I know what she needs, where we have to go to help her lose her fear.

"Why do you have that?" Mia asks. She tries to put a hard edge in her voice, but the waver at the end gives her away.

"You have a fear of guns," I say. "We need to get you past that."

"It's a good fear," she says. "Guns kill people. You said it yourself. There's no antidote to a bullet." She glances down at the handle. "Especially those."

"It's not my weapon of choice," I say. And it's true. "But we will have them pointed at us on a daily basis, in this line of work." I lift the gun, remove the magazine, and clear the chamber. I set the bullets on the bedside table.

She comes forward with trepidation, watching the magazine as if it might leap back into the gun.

"Come sit," I say.

She obeys me, propping anxiously on the edge of the bed. I double-check the chamber, then place the gun in her lap. Her eyes lock on to the gleaming metal. She doesn't move to hold it.

"Give me your wrists," I say.

When she looks up at me, her eyes widen at the length of dark pink rope in my hand. Then they go back to the gun.

I move to stand in front of her. She lifts her hands up. The gun starts to slide down her lap, and she yelps and lifts her knees.

"Good, good," I tell her. I wrap the rope around both her wrists in smooth, even turns. Then I create a whipping knot between them. They are lashed together like handcuffs now.

Her eyes don't leave the gun. I pick it up from her lap and pull on the end of the rope, lifting her hands above her head. The movement makes a delicious shift in her breasts, those pert nipples rising, straining against the blue film of the fabric.

I ice down my control and lash the end of the rope to the slats in the bed. She can escape this easily, if she chooses to. My job is to make sure she doesn't want to.

I slide one hand beneath her and shift her to lie down on the bed. When she's in a comfortable position, I trail my hand from her bound wrist, to her shoulder, then trace the curve of that lovely breast.

She sucks in a breath. I give her what she's longing for, trapping that tight nipple between my finger and thumb. She moans as I roll it gently.

I lean down to take her lips with mine. She is eager, hungry, as we connect with mouths and tongues. While I have her attention elsewhere, I touch the gun to her thigh.

She breaks the kiss, flinching from the chill. Her breathing speeds up against my mouth, her lips no longer moving. I bite her lower lip and tweak the nipple again.

She's caught, I can tell, between the pleasure and the panic. But this is good. It means I can coax the terror away.

I let the gun trail down her thigh. She relaxes a little, but I can still feel the tension, coiled and ready to spring again.

Her mouth moves against mine. I linger for another moment, then slide down her jaw, her neck, and farther, to capture that plump nipple between my teeth.

She moans again and arches into me. I blow hot air over the fabric, heating it.

Mia lifts her hips, trying to establish contact between us down below. I smile around her breast. Such exquisitely sweet torture.

The gun slips against her ribs and she halts again. But it's less of an intrusion this time, and soon she resumes rocking up against me.

"Good girl," I whisper.

I need her skin, so I lift the nightie. When my mouth closes over her breast again, she lurches up, a cry escaping.

I move the gun lower and let it connect with her between her legs.

Her eyes pop open in surprise. She watches me and looks down, fascinated at what I might do.

She doesn't show any fear of it at all now.

"You like that?" I ask. I push it harder against her, feeling it engage between the folds, pressing her panties into her skin.

"You're crazy," she says.

"Mmmm." I lift the gun a little, then let it slide inside the top edge of the blue satin.

She takes in another breath. The metal is warm now, heated by her skin. I press it into her a little harder, letting it engage with her body.

She moans. "This is so messed up," she says.

"I think I've made my point," I tell her. I begin to withdraw it from her.

But she tightens her knees. "Do it," she says. "I want to push boundaries with you."

My entire body responds to this and it's all I can do not to rip off the panties and thrust inside her.

But I tighten my jaw and do as she asks, peeling her panties down with the barrel of the gun.

Her gaze is riveted on it. I touch her myself to make sure she can handle this. Her body rises up to meet my fingers as I slide inside. She's so wet. And vibrating with need.

Now I'm the one who feels the anxiety as I press the barrel gently against her skin. Jesus. I hadn't pictured going this direction.

I glance up at her, the blue negligee pushed high and exposing her body, her arms tied above her head. She watches me with desire and wicked delight. "Nervous?" she asks.

I slide only the tip of the barrel inside her. I'm so damn erect I feel like I'm going to explode. She's pink and wet and the blue metal going into her threatens to send me over the edge.

She spreads her knees wide and lifts up. Hell, I can barely manage this, slipping the barrel back out and letting it enter her again. Her body quivers with the movement. She isn't watching any longer. Her chin is high, her body tense. I can tell she's moving toward orgasm.

I can't take it any longer and pull the gun away, shoving it across the bed. I enter her in one swift stroke.

Her body heaves against me, rocking. She's moaning and crying out and mixing up my first name and my last. I hold on to her hips, driving into her, relishing the feel of her convulsions around me.

We move together, the world completely erased, then I empty into her, my body flush against hers. I wrap my arms around her back and clasp her to my chest.

The ropes hit my head and I realize she's gotten them loose. Her arms come down and clutch at me.

I hold on to her, and her to me, until our bodies settle. I kiss her neck.

"You got over it," I whisper into her ear.

"I did," she says.

For the first time in over a year, since before Ridley Prison, before the night I killed Singer, and before I knew what a traitor I had allowed into my heart with Jovana, I actually smile. A real, genuine, non-sardonic, actual smile.

Shit. I think I've fallen in love with this woman.

20

MIA

It's still dark outside when I wake. I try not to move. Jax is asleep, and he will jump into fight stance at the drop of a pin. I wonder if that comes from Vigilante training, or if he's just naturally like that.

He's so vulnerable looking in sleep. I can't see much, just the shadows of his face from the glow of the alarm clock. But it tugs at my heart. I don't know how he can live like this, wary and suspicious all the time.

Maybe it's just our situation. A normal Vigilante probably has breaks between missions. And if he was a director, there were probably days of paperwork as much as car chases and bullet dodging.

I think back on last night and the gun. I shudder a little. Something I haven't told Jax, but will soon, is that since seeing the gun, I remember a piece of my past that must have been long buried.

I'm on a boat with my parents. I think I'm six, maybe seven. My mother is out on the deck, holding on to the rail. My dad is in front at the controls. This is a typical weekend for us off the coast of Miami.

Mom is watching something through binoculars. I don't know what she's looking at. The water and sky seem unbroken to me. After a moment, she comes and takes my hand and calmly tells me to go below deck.

We head down a little ladder. She gives me a puzzle and asks me to stay here a minute. She'll be right back.

But something in her tone worries me. I feel funny inside, a little buzz in my belly like something is wrong.

She heads back up and through the door. I start

on the puzzle, but the boat makes a turn and we must be speeding up, because the pieces slide off the table.

The motor roars. My anxiety rises, wondering why we're in a hurry. I creep up the ladder and push on the door, peering out to see if I can spot Mom.

Nobody is on deck. I lift it a little more and look around toward the front cabin. My dad and my mom are gesturing at each other. They look upset. My dad is holding something. I can't make out what it is. Mom takes it from him, and then I know.

It's a gun.

A gun!

I drop the hatch and scramble back down the ladder.

I never remember feeling more afraid than at that moment.

I crawl onto a beanbag chair and curl up in a ball, shaking and trying not to cry.

Eventually my mom comes down again. The boat slows down. She calmly picks up the puzzle pieces and starts arranging them. She asks me if I'm tired.

I tell her I'm not and get up to help with the puzzle. I don't ask about the gun, because then she'll know I disobeyed her and went up the ladder. But the fear remains.

Lying in bed next to Jax, I swallow hard. I know the incident doesn't have to mean anything. It could point to them being Vigilantes, and that's why I ended up at a safe house. Or it could just be an element of who they were, a part I didn't get a chance to know. Maybe they were just afraid of a boat coming at them too suddenly.

But in my heart, I start to believe something I've held so tightly that I haven't faced it until now. Jax's world is where I came from. I didn't get old enough to be told. And my aunt — if she really was my aunt — didn't want me involved.

I mentally flip through the photo albums from my house. Were there pictures of my mother and my aunt together?

Yes, I can remember one standing next to each other by a boat. A few others at parties.

But I have nothing of the two of them together as children. And nothing of my grandparents. I never knew them. We didn't have pictures.

Suddenly I find it hard to believe that all four of my grandparents are dead. I saw my parents in their coffins. I know they are gone.

But I never knew any of my grandparents. They died before I was born, or so I was told.

Something isn't right here. That's too much death. This doesn't happen to normal families.

I want to wake Jax up, get him to look up my parents' parents. I don't know if he feels the rising tension in me, but his eyes open. He's awake instantly, sitting up, scanning the room. "What is it?" he asks. "Did you hear something?"

I put my hand on his arm. "No. I was just thinking."

He relaxes back down. "What about?"

"I remembered something about my parents. On our boat. With a gun."

He draws me in close. "So you're starting to think they weren't as ordinary as you have always believed?"

"Can we look them up? Or my grandparents? Why don't I have any grandparents? Or pictures of my family when they were children? I never really thought about it, assuming the images were lost when my parents died and I moved to my aunt's. But now, I wonder."

"Your information is locked up tight," he says. "But I can try."

I lay my head on his shoulder. "Thank you," I tell him. Emotion courses through me. I know we're in terrible danger and that sometime later today, we'll have to go to Washington and face everything. We might not survive it. Or we might get separated and I won't even know if Jax is killed.

I might never see him again, nor be told what happened.

Like with my family.

But there is nothing to do but go into it, just go.

For the first time in days, I feel like crying, overwhelmed with fear of what is to come. Jax seems to know it's happening, and kisses my hair. "They haven't gotten us yet," he says.

It's true. We've come through everything.

"I'm scared," I admit.

"Fear is natural," he says. "It's how we perform in spite of our fear that sets us apart."

I lift my face and he kisses me, light and gentle. My body starts to warm up, a light humming coming over me. His hand comes behind my back to roll me closer. We're still naked, and his skin is hot.

"Come here," he says, and guides my leg over him.

My thigh brushes his erection, and I go from

warm to flaming in one fevered rush. I settle my knees on either side of his hips, and lower myself down. No preamble. No startup. Just straight inside.

Sparks fly through my body as he fills me. His hands hold my waist, then travel up to cup my breasts. I lift and lower at my own pace, taking him in easy. Every stroke is like a revelation, a new plane of ecstasy.

The first glow of morning strikes the window, and I can see him a little better, watching me from the pillow. I brace my hands on his chest and speed up my pace. It's building so fast, and I can't control it. I just ride along with the rhythm set by my body, the direction and speed it is longing for.

Then it begins, a tightening of my muscles around him, a thrumming sensation vibrating through me. It's steady and predictable at first, spreading out. Then everything just bursts. The orgasm explodes out, reaching all the way to the roots of my hair. I cry out, saying words, an endless stream of endearments and exclamations. Jax clutches my hips, thrusting to my pace, then holds tight as he flows into me.

I feel his arms shake as we keep this position, shattered, fulfilled, and both undoubtedly a little afraid that this is it, that one or both of us won't see another morning rise up from the horizon.

I collapse on his chest and bury my face in his neck. His arms come around me and he holds me tight. "It will be all right," he whispers.

My voice won't work, so I say nothing. The sun keeps coming. No one, not even Jax, can keep it from rising and making this day begin.

21

JAX

I listen to the soft hiss of the shower in the bathroom as I dress. In my mind I picture the rivulets of water cascading down Mia's body, caressing each curve as my own fingers have often done so recently. For a moment I envy them. They are ephemeral, however, a fleeting touch on her skin. Perhaps they should be jealous of me.

I sit on the edge of the bed and pull out the Identipad. Mia's record is easy to recall from the cache without pinging a Vigilante server. It still tells me nothing more than it did that first night. Just a name.

I let my idle gaze wander the room as I think about how to find out more, and I spot the black onyx ring sitting on the nightstand. I pick it up and turn it in my fingers. Inside the band are the initials we found last night. KHS.

I decide to risk a connection and pull up the Vigilante network on the Identipad after bouncing the signal through as many anonymizer nodes as I can find. It won't stop someone if they're looking, but it will slow them down. Then I let the Identipad scan the ring, and I start digging.

Currently the ring has only a special's ID attached to it, which means there is no way of getting a name for the current owner. The initials are a dead end, but a query into the history gets some hits. It's old, dating back to the founding of the Vigilantes during World War II.

But still no names. I idly flip through early records and stop on a grainy black-and-white photo of several early Vigilantes. They're posing in front of what looks like the Lincoln Memorial in Washington, D.C. The man on the far left has one arm around his neighbor, and the other clutching his suit. Prominent on his right hand is a large black ring.

I check the names. The man on the right is Mr. Prescott Adams. I pull up his information and scan through photos.

There's no doubt. The black ring is his. But whose initials are inside the ring? They aren't his.

I type in his name in the network. He's a special, which isn't surprising since the ring is tagged as belonging to one. I glance at the identification number and blink, looking at it again.

000001.

He's the first Vigilante. The first special.

But his ID is not the one connected to the ring now.

My heart speeds up. I have a hunch. A crazy, wild, unbelievable hunch.

I pull up recent records from the St. Louis silo and skim the information. Somewhere among all the alerts surrounding me is what I'm looking for.

I suck in a breath when I find it. A number. The ID number of the only special who entered the silo on the same day I did.

Mia.

I cross-reference that number with the one

currently tied to the ring.

It's a match.

I'm dumbfounded. No wonder they protect her. No wonder she has the key to everything.

She's a Vigilante. And not from just any Vigilante family.

The very first one.

My head buzzes. This explains so many things. The safe house. Her aunt. Her parents, and the gun on the boat. And all the wiped records surrounding them.

But how do I tell her?

A noise from beyond the closed door pulls me from my thoughts. I check the time. Too early for the bartender to show up, and any other staff would have announced themselves.

Not good. I scout the room for defendable positions and weapons. No telling where the gun is. Somewhere on the floor, under the bed. Out of reach. I grab the rope we used last night. I can work with this.

I jump from the bed as the bedroom door swings open on silent hinges. Two men fill the doorway, one standing and one crouched low, dart throwers in their hands. I catch a glimpse of a woman behind them.

No mistaking Vigilantes.

"Please don't," says the standing man, motioning at the rope in my hands. "We really don't want to involve Ms. Morrow."

I look at the bathroom door. The shower is still running.

"She's fine. And alone," says the woman from behind the two men. "But we are not." The implication is clear. The building is surrounded. And I'm trapped.

For the moment.

I sit back down on the bed. The rope and ring are still in my hands. I need to stall long enough to come up with a plan. "I expected you sooner."

The woman looks bemused and tosses me a shirt. I guess I'm leaving in my pajama pants. "We didn't want to interrupt your romantic interactions," she says.

The crouching man snickers, and she nudges him into silence.

"And that's why you haven't shot me yet, despite the standing kill order."

She nods. "Our orders were to take you away from the special first. We'll take care of the messy parts soon enough."

"I'm sure you don't want your lady in danger," the crouching man says.

If they are even entertaining the idea of involving her, then they have no clue how special Mia really is. I do not doubt the hell they would go through if any harm befell her. Accidents happen, however. And with Sutherland calling the shots, a cover-up would be a certainty.

A sick feeling forms in my belly. The longer I stall, the greater the chance she gets hurt.

Or worse.

I can't risk it. But I can't just vanish on her.

"Very well," I say. "I will go with you. On one condition." The woman raises her eyebrows but says nothing, waiting. I start tying a simple knot around the ring. "Mia's gotten wrapped up in this circus surrounding me. I must know she will be safe and protected once I'm out of the picture."

"She's a special, of course she will be," says the woman.

"Not good enough. You know her house was blown up. That wasn't just about me."

The woman's eyes harden for a second, as if she thinks I'm accusing her of something. But just as quickly, they soften.

"I saw the report," she says. "No one is supposed to harm the special, but some people took matters into their own hands." She snorts. "The official cause is 'undetermined.'" Her expression makes clear that she knows it's a cover-up.

"So you see my concern," I say.

"Killing her is not part of our job today," the woman says. "Now, move."

The shower shuts off. I glance at the bathroom door, then back to the woman. She watches me, then gives me a small smile. "Time to go," she mouths silently. She kicks my shoes at me.

I think about going into a full-scale battle. Fight them off to the last minute. My fists tighten. Even if they dart-gun me, I'll have several minutes to do damage.

But if Mia comes out, she could get caught in the crossfire.

Crouching man seems to know what I'm thinking. He heads over to the window and pulls back the curtain.

There's a window washer there with his wide metal shelf. He waves at me, then opens his jacket. A normal gun, metallic blue, like Klaus's.

They'll shoot me on site, then. And Mia would have to come out and find the mess. I don't want that.

I shove my shoes on my feet and walk to the door. The two men stand aside, weapons at the ready, but I keep my stance open and nonthreatening. They fall in behind me as the woman leads us out. I resist the urge to look back. It wouldn't do any good.

At least my last memories of Mia will be happy.

22

Mia

I wipe a circle from the steam fogging up the bathroom mirror. The girl looking back at me seems more confident than I remember. More full of hope.

"We're going to get through this," I whisper to her. "And we're going to kick some ass doing it."

I rub my head with a towel as I survey the outfit I picked out for today's upcoming mission. Armond is a magician with clothes. Black leather pants, a dark gray turtleneck sweater, and a sweet black jacket with a furry inset on the collar.

The jacket has a million zippered pockets on the outside, and a couple hidden ones inside. "Spy gadget central," I tell it as I merrily zip and unzip a few of the compartments. I hold it in front of me and turn back to the mirror. "And I'll look good doing it."

"The shower's all yours!" I call to the other room. I was a little pouty when Jax hung back as I headed to the bathroom. I thought he might want to come in with me. But he was stony and serious, no doubt concerned about traveling and what would happen when we arrived in Washington.

I'm all about the minute-to-minute. I stare hard at myself in the mirror, which is rapidly clearing of steam. "You might die today," I tell myself seriously.

But my heart doesn't feel it. Jax is unstoppable. Nobody gets the better of him.

"When do we need to leave?" I ask loudly.

Still no response.

I wrap the towel tightly around me and head into the bedroom to see why he hasn't answered me.

The bedroom is empty. Strange.

I head out into the living room. Not there. Nor the dining area. He's left?

My heart starts to quicken. There's something not right about the room. The impression of other people. A sense of invasion.

The front door is shut tight. The windows closed.

But I sense it.

"Jax?" I call out one more time, fear blooming. I race back to the bedroom. His suitcase is still here. The clothes he wore yesterday, neatly folded on the chair. Even the knapsack with his binoculars weapon and the Blackphone, the untraceable one with no contacts.

I hunt through his suitcase. All the clothes are new, so I don't know what he might have taken with him. But why leave his weapons and tech? For me? He'll have everything in his car.

I threw his phone in the parking lot. The one here is blank. I can't contact him.

Why did he leave me? Is he really going to Washington without me?

I sit on the bed, tears threatening. After all my self-pep talks, I'm totally bereft. I thought we were doing this thing together.

Something bumps against my thigh. It's the black oval ring. Our bondage rope is tied to it. It's nothing special. Just a silly plain ol' square knot.

"Good job, Jax," I say bitterly. "Leave me with the knot every kid learns in kindergarten."

I turn the ring over in my hand, my eyes burning. At least the ring is mine and was always mine. It's something I still have of my life, my house.

I tug on the string to untie the knot.

Then I realize something.

It's not a square knot at all.

It's a thief knot. It's a trick of sorts. Sailors would use it to know if someone had opened their trunks and then tied them closed again. The thief wouldn't know that the knot wasn't a normal one, but this special kind.

The kind that sends the message — something's been stolen.

Jax!

He's been taken by the Vigilantes!

I don't even panic. I've faced too many things in too short a time to let that happen anymore.

Be systematic, make a plan, and think everything through, I tell myself.

I go back to the bathroom, dress quickly, and tie my hair back.

If I had greasepaint, I'd totally put it under my eyes like a linebacker before a football game.

But instead, I choose the easiest bag to carry, a soft leather backpack, and load up all the weapons and Vigilante tech in the room, a clean shirt, and just as a measure of comfort, the blue nightie.

The girl in the mirror looks wary now, ready to do hard business. I snatch up the UFC ball cap Jax wore to the fight last night and shove it on my head, bringing the rim down low.

I strap the backpack on and head out of the room. I know I can't go to Jax's car. Either the Vigilantes have it or they've rigged it so that it will be useless to me. Or track me.

But I know something they probably don't.

I have another car. The one in Alpine that Jax and I left when he realized I had his Aston Martin.

I'll get the Acura we stole, drive to Alpine, and get to that car. Once I have it, I'll contact Sam, or Colette, or even Armond. Get back in the game. I'll take that damn car right up to the silo in Missouri, if I have to. I'll drive right through the damn doors.

Yes.

I feel strong and fierce as I head out into the bright morning. I know where the car is. Despite all our circular driving last night after getting away, it's only about five miles. I'll walk it. And pay attention.

I still have the cash Jovana shoved at me last night, so I stop along the way for a breakfast sandwich and coffee. Sustenance. Rest. Alertness.

I'm on this.

The city is full of sunshine and schoolchildren and people heading to work. It's hard to pass them by, knowing my life is turned upside down while theirs goes on normally.

Do the Vigilantes really keep these people safe? Everything I've seen so far leads me to believe they have serious internal problems. But I know so little.

Time for me to get up close and personal.

I tug the brim of the cap to keep it right over my eyes and pay attention to every car that passes. I nickname them based on their color and license plate so that I will notice any of them that repeat. JAYthree Blue. Ugly brown PZazz. White van KTycat.

So far, so good.

It takes an hour to get there. I approach the parking lot with care. It's situated behind an office building. Last night, it was full of cars that arrived too late to get in the official arena parking. Today, it bustles with office workers.

It's late enough by now that there aren't any people wandering around. I hold my breath that the Acura is still where we left it.

I'm sorely tempted to check the bush where I threw Jax's phone, but there's no point in using it even if it's still there. They could track that in an instant. The Acura is a safe bet. It belongs to someone else entirely.

And it's still parked in the corner in the shadow of the building.

I glance left and right. A man comes out of the back door of the complex, talking on his cell phone. I slow my step, letting him get into his car and drive away before I approach the Acura.

The car is low slung, shorter than me. The skeleton key Jax used to open it is still on the outside. I am anxious to open the door. If it's locked, I won't know what to punch to get it open.

I reach out with shaking fingers and pull on the handle.

It opens.

I let out a sigh of relief. Now I just have to endure the drive back to Alpine, get the other car, and be on my way back to Jax.

I won't accept any plan other than one that leads me back to him.

I pull my backpack off my shoulders and lean in to toss it on the passenger seat.

Except someone is sitting there.

Someone in a skirt.

I look up. The woman is holding out a watch. A Vigilante watch.

Her watch.

"You left this in the car," she says. "So easy to track."

She points a gun at me. "Now drive."

It's Jovana.

You've reached the end of Vigilante's Lover #3!

It's the last cliffie!
The series will end with #4.

Come ~~scream~~ talk about the cliffhangers
on Facebook with Annie's Vigilantes:

www.facebook.com/groups/anniesvigilantes

Join the mail list to make sure
you don't miss a release!

www.anniewinters.com

Annie has continued her grand tradition of killer
endings that began with her work as JJ Knight. Fans
don't call her the Queen of Cliffhangers for nothing!

Annie and Tony are modeling *Vigilante* after the
structure of television suspense series. We release
very quickly so you don't have long to wait!